SEASIDE SUNRISE

NELLIE BROOKS

Merpaper Press

Cover design by: Nellie Brooks

ISBN-13: 978-1-958957-01-1

CONTENTS

CHAPTER 1

Mela pulled a honey frame from the beehive and held it into the sunlight. The heavy comb was as golden as the August afternoon, and the sweet scent of wax mingled with the fragrance of the wildflowers growing on the bluff.

"Would you mind holding the frame for me, Peter?" Mela leaned and peered into the hive. It was hard to see much in the dark, let alone spot the queen. The rows of frames hanging in the box were teeming with bees, but as long as Mela moved gently and puffed smoke, they wouldn't sting. Even if they did... Luckily, Mela had inherited her mother's beekeeping genes and barely reacted to the venom.

She looked up. "Peter?"

Her partner eyed the frame. "There's no place that's not covered with bees." Even though Peter was a wildlife biologist and faced apex predators without twitching an eye, handling honeybees unnerved him. He adjusted his veil, his sapphire eyes squinting in frustration behind the netting. "I can't get a grip."

Mela smiled fondly at him. So what if she was freshly divorced and they were both getting on in years? Peter was the kindest man she knew, and he'd loved her all his life.

It had taken her much longer to find out that she, too, loved him.

The frame weighed a good five pounds. Mela's arm started to tremble. "This colony is particularly sweet," she promised. "Besides, if they sting you, they die, and they're as eager to see the next day as anyone else. Just sort of wiggle your fingers in between without squishing them." She cleared the smile from her throat. "There are beekeeping gloves too. They're thick leather and go up your arms if you want to—"

"Gloves? Pffft, those are for... I can do it. I can do it." Peter's chest expanded with a bracing breath. He gingerly grasped the frame with forceps-fingers, pinkie sticking out as far as it would go, and lifted the frame. "See? No problem." He sounded surprised.

"Very good. Let me just check for Her Majesty." Mela quickly scanned the frame. Even if everyone else was lifting off and leaving and coming back, the queen was the one bee Mela needed to stay. "All right. She's not on here." There were only baby bees, their fur still fuzzy and plush instead of rubbed thin from dipping in and out of flowers.

"They seem annoyed," Peter observed.

"Reasonable. They were peacefully capping honey and dreaming of flowers. We pulled them from the cozy dark into the bright sunlight; it's a bit of an outrage."

"You sure the queen's not there?" Peter turned the frame over, inspecting the other side. He was getting the hang of it, no longer minding the workers crawling on his hands. "Honestly, they all look the same."

"She's marked with a hot pink paint dot. And she's big." Mela picked up her double-ended hive tool. It was red on the hook side and black on the chisel side and, in her opinion, the most useful tool known to humanity. It also held sentimental value. Her mother Julie gave it to Mela when she turned ten years old.

Shortly after that birthday, Julie and her brother, Finn, were lost at sea. For all anyone knew, there'd been an accident; probably something to do with the boat Finn had built.

Nothing—and nobody—had ever been found, yet the adults in Mela's life had been quick to put it together. The police had confirmed that a freak current was to blame. Case closed. Decades later, the lack of evidence still lodged like a stinging burr in Mela's mind.

Using the dull blade of the tool, Mela scraped away wax and propolis. Her gaze brushed a crawling bee, and she stopped.

Something wasn't quite right.

Mela leaned to see better, holding her breath. Buried in the bee's fur was a small reddish-brown mite. It looked like a minuscule tick, and Mela was about as glad to see it. "Shoot," she whispered.

"What?" Peter lowered the frame.

"Oh—nothing." Mela picked the wax off her tool's blade. "There's a bee with a mite. And...yep. There's another."

Peter put his face next to hers. Despite the veil between them, it gave Mela more of a thrill than opening a nest of twenty thousand stinging insects.

"That tiny dot?" he asked, seemingly unaware of how much he was distracting her. "Looks harmless enough."

"It does. But that tiny dot can be big trouble," Mela said. "They're called Varroa mites, and I don't like spotting them so casually. I had better check the colonies."

"Should've checked before you bought them," Peter said sternly, but when she huffed impatiently, he gently bumped his shoulder into hers. "Just kidding. I'm surprised you saw that itty-bitty thing at all."

Mela had bought the bees from an old beekeeper on impulse only a month before and didn't know much about them. Most beekeepers treated their colonies routinely for parasites and diseases, but some people and some treatments were more effective than others.

"What do I do with this?" Peter interrupted her thoughts, holding up the frame in his hands.

"You can put it in there," she said and nodded at a small box on the ground. "I'm going to give the colony empty frames. They've run out of space to store honey, poor things."

She lifted a brand-new frame from the box. Unlike the full frame, this one held only a thin sheet of pre-stamped lines in the shape of hexagons. The bees would use the stamps as the foundation for building their cells.

They swapped a few more frames, Mela puffed the last cloud of burlap smoke to calm the colony, and then she closed the hive.

Peter carried the boxes to his blue vintage Chevy truck while Mela gathered tools and extinguished the smoldering smoker. Then she, too, waded through the knee-deep grass to the street and loaded her equipment onto the truck.

"All done." She poured water from a bottle over her sticky, smoky hands. "Did you have fun?"

Far from the hives, Peter untied the strings of his veil and tossed it on the truck bed. "I did. But I'm also glad it's over and we survived." He pulled her close and gave her a long kiss.

After a marriage that had cooled years before it ended, Peter's love was a gift—unexpected and precious.

When he was done kissing her, he turned Mela so she leaned into his chest, wrapped his arms around her, and put his chin on her head. "Look," he murmured.

They stood, looking over the waving grass that was sprinkled with colorful flowers and half-hidden hives. The sea and sky, as blue as hydrangeas, perfected the picture.

Mela lost herself in the beauty of the coast and the warm, safe feeling of Peter's embrace until a guilty thought niggled its way to the front.

She should check on Sunny.

Sunny was—possibly, probably—Julie's half sister and Mela's aunt. She was also elderly, had lost her house and possessions in a landslide, and suffered from an old hip injury. Mela had found her at the ramshackle Bay Harbor Motel Peter inherited from his father, and when she asked Sunny to move into Julie's beach house with her, the old lady gladly accepted.

"I should go home," Mela said and tilted her head to look at Peter.

"I know." He smiled.

"What about you?" she asked. Peter was renovating the motel, mostly by himself. His father had thoroughly run the business into the ground, and until it would attract tourists again, Peter's lifetime savings were draining away at a breathtaking rate.

He tightened his hold, bringing his mouth to her ear. "I know you worry about the motel," he murmured. "Don't. I'm fixing it up. But I don't want it to be all I'm doing. I've been waiting thirty years for you, so let me enjoy your company."

Mela turned in his arms and kissed him again. She was still finding her way in the relationship but compared to her marriage, this was *easy*. There were no wrong paths, only different ones. In the end, they all led her to Peter.

"All right, all right, all right," he said when she let him go, and it made her laugh.

"Do you have a moment for me to pick a bouquet?" she asked.

"As long as I don't have to help," he replied and opened his arms to free her.

"I'll be quick," she promised. A few steps into the field, and she was surrounded by every single kind of flower blooming on the coast of Maine.

Mela gathered a big armful of black-eyed Susans, lupines, and Queen Anne's lace, and then she returned to Peter, who was sitting on the open bed of his Chevy with a bottle of water.

He grinned when he saw her bounty and poured the rest of the water over his head. "Think you have enough there?" He shook the drops from his eyes and jumped down.

"Barely," Mela said critically. "I'm going to make big bouquets for you and Amelie, and smaller ones for my daughters' rooms."

Amelie was her best friend and should definitely have flowers. Kimmie and Sisley, Mela's daughters, also needed something to cheer them up. Kimmie was in the process of buying a foreclosure in Bay Harbor, and Sisley, very pregnant, had just escaped her abusive relationship. "Oh. And Sunny needs one for the kitchen."

Peter pulled a ball cap from the back pocket of his jeans and slapped it on his head. "Talking about Sunny—I meant to finish the window in her room today. I also want to check on the closet in the nursery. I can hear over at the motel when Sisley closes that door. Let's go, beautiful."

Mela hitched her flowers higher in her arms and climbed into the truck's passenger seat. Peter closed her door and secured the truck bed, then sat in the driver's seat and let the truck rumble to life.

"Peter," Mela said as they pulled off the bumpy field into the also bumpy, unpaved alley. Dry dust whirled where the wheels met the ground, and Mela cranked her window higher.

"Yes." He shifted into a higher gear.

"I know you want me to be happy, and I am. But I don't want to take too much of your time. You've got your own things to do at the motel."

"I know." He glanced at her. "You've told me about a hundred times. And what did I tell you, my darling?"

"You told me that *you* decide how you spend your time," she replied politely.

"Do you think that's a good idea?"

"Yes," she said. "Of course it is. It's just..."

"Don't you dare yes-but me," he growled, making her laugh. He stopped and shook his head. "Listen, you don't need to worry about me. Managing your husband was your last job, and that's over. The two of us are a whole different ball game."

She'd managed Robert's political career for years—until she realized he didn't need her anymore. In the end she'd done it only because it had become second nature, a skin she discovered she didn't actually like wearing. Mela sighed. "Okay."

"I know you're good at it," he said and rubbed her arm. "But I want *you*. Not your skill set."

"Right." She leaned her head on his shoulder. It was fine that there were no electric windows or air conditioning. The old truck made up plenty by having a single bench in front instead of separate seats.

They drove through the empty, sunny streets of Bay Harbor until they reached 12 Seasweet Lane.

The house was blue with a slanted shingle roof and sat at the end of the street, surrounded by flowers and the remnants of an old apple orchard.

Every time Mela returned here, even if she'd been gone for only half an hour, she thrilled at seeing the blooming front yard, at knowing that in the back, the patio and garden of her childhood still looked out at the sea.

She loved the house, the coast, the sandy path winding down to the beach. Every stick was an old friend here, every blade of grass a comfort, every sunrise familiar. The old honey barn in the orchard was not a dilapidated shed but a beloved playground, and though the trees made few apples anymore, they tasted as sweet and crisp as the decades of experience that grew them.

The front door opened, and Sunny appeared, waving. Behind her, Kimmie's edgy pixie cut bobbed into view.

"Hi!" Mela jumped out of the truck and went to them, blowing air kisses and scattering petals in her wake. "How lovely to come home to a greeting like that!"

She hugged her daughter, squeezing her tight. Kimmie lived a risky life as an investigative journalist, and Mela made the most out of their time together.

"Hi, Mom." Kimmie returned the hug. Hugs, especially long ones, were strictly a Bay Harbor thing for her. She'd been eight when she last allowed them, but something in the salty air softened her.

"Hi, sweetheart." From the corner of her eye, Mela spotted Peter awkwardly patting Sunny's arm. Mela swallowed a smile. The two tended to express their significant mutual sympathy mostly through cheese sandwiches and stories. Sunny nodded that she was okay, and Peter stepped back, looking relieved.

"Kimmie, do you want to help me unload the honey?" Peter asked. "It should go into the barn before the wax melts."

"Sure! Only...Sunny?" Kimmie nudged the old lady.

"Look what came, Mela." Sunny pulled an envelope from the pocket of her voluminous tunic and nervously waved it in the air. "It's the test results."

"They came." Mela took the envelope. Suddenly, the flowers in her arm weighed a ton, the pricks and scratches from stems and leaves making her itch with nerves.

Peter put a hand on her shoulder. "It'll be all right," he said reassuringly. Then he winked at Kimmie. "What do you say, kid? It'd be good to get the frames into the shade."

"Got it." Officially on vacation, Kimmie was dressed in jeans shorts and a red checkered blouse knotted midriff. It was a stark contrast to her usual urban-warfare garb and a skimpy outfit for hauling heavy wooden boxes. But Kimmie was tough. Undaunted, she scooted past Sunny, companionably bumped Mela with her hip, and then followed Peter to the truck.

Mela dropped the flowers into the grass and took Sunny's arm.

"I've gotten used to thinking of you as my niece, but there's the final word." Sunny pointed at the sealed test results. "I'm nervous."

"Me too," Mela admitted, fanning herself with the envelope. "Let's go sit on the patio and read the verdict."

CHAPTER 2

The patio was surrounded by a garden, and the garden was surrounded by an old, low stone wall. Beyond the wall, an unmowed field sloped to a beach that met the sea.

Sunny groaned as she lowered herself into one of the wide wicker chairs. "Oof. Sometimes I really feel like an old woman."

Mela put the envelope on the table and weighed it down with a large shell. "I'm just going to wash and get us something to drink," she said. "Give me one second."

She wanted Sunny to get better—the woman was not yet seventy. Mentally, she was as fit as ever. Only the hip was holding her back. Sunny never complained, even though she'd lost everything from her house to her health insurance. But she was hurting. Not only from chronic pain but also from years of being unable to do what she liked. It was hard to think of all the beach walks she'd missed.

Inside, Mela took a minute to wash her face and hands and change her sweaty shirt for a fresh linen blouse. Back downstairs, she filled a pitcher with ice cubes and lemonade and brought it outside, then returned for glasses, plates, and the chocolate pistachio key-lime pie Amelie had dropped off in the morning.

Amelie baked for relaxation the way other people ate potato chips in front of the TV. The more she baked, the harder she claimed it was to stop.

"Scrumptious as it looks, I can't eat a bite until I know what that letter says," Sunny said when Mela handed her a plate with a slice. She put it on the table. "Go ahead. Let's get it over with."

"Okay." Mela inhaled and picked up the envelope. It looked like a bill, but it was from the genetic testing lab. After piecing together that Sunny might be Julie's half sister and Mela's aunt, Sunny and Mela had sent their DNA to be analyzed.

"Isn't it weird how little we know about Finn?" Mela said, aware she was stalling. Talking about her uncle was a good way to stall. There was a strange absence of information. Julie had jotted few notes about Finn in her journal, Grandma Constance had never mentioned him at all, and Sunny had met him only once, to quickly admire his half-build boat before Julie whisked her away again.

Mela had met her uncle when he visited but knew next to nothing about him. Not even whether he had been older or younger than Julie—it simply hadn't occurred to her to ask. She wished she had.

"You're stalling," Sunny said. "Don't. My stomach can't take it."

Mela picked up her cake fork and slid the handle under the flap. "Either way the results don't change anything. You're still living with me."

Sunny nodded.

With a nervous flourish, Mela opened the envelope and pulled out the sheet of paper, her eyes flying over the few lines. "Where does it—here. Yes!" She looked up, beaming.

Sunny looked like she wanted to cry. "Yes?"

"Yes! You're Julie's half sister! You're my aunt!" Mela jumped up and threw her arms around Sunny.

Sunny hugged Mela back, holding on tight. "Julie was my sister," she said, sounding stunned. "I knew it! I had a sister and a brother. And you, baby girl—you're my niece. My actual niece."

Mela nodded, not trusting her voice. After Julie's disappearance she'd been adopted, but only after spending many years in the foster system. Now, almost forty years later, by the sheer grace of good luck, she had found her family.

"I was Julie's *friend*." Sunny's hands trembled where she held Mela. "Can you believe it? She died so young, and still I found her in time to be her friend. Do you think it was a coincidence?"

"No," Mela said, her voice muffled because she couldn't let go of her aunt. "It was not. It was your right to love each other. Grandma Constance couldn't keep you apart."

Sunny sobbed a laugh and then she let go to shift into a more comfortable position in her chair. "I only wish I would have known Finn too. Julie mentioned him sometimes, but she never said much."

"Yes." Mela straightened her back. She'd known she was right. But to have her guess officially confirmed—it felt different. Better.

"I guess that's a yes?" Kimmie came from the barn, her checkered blouse streaked with beeswax and smoker soot. Peter followed closely behind.

Mela wanted to call out to them and share the news, but she only managed a small sound before tears suddenly streamed down her face.

She wiped her sleeve over her cheeks and laughed at all the feelings welling up, then pulled Kimmie into a hug. "You have a certified great-aunt."

Kimmie, hard-boiled reporter that she was, squealed and hugged Mela back.

Peter took Sunny's hand. Mela saw the relieved glance he gave his old friend. Then Kimmie went to her great-aunt, and Peter came to Mela.

"Congratulations," he said quietly. "I really hoped it was true. For your sake—and even more for Sunny's. Having a family means everything." He stopped and cleared his throat.

Kimmie kissed Sunny's cheek and put a hand on her aunt's shoulder. "Are you two sharing that pie?" she asked. "Seems like a celebration is in order."

Peter's eyes crinkled. "Your mom brought out plenty of plates," he said. "Do you want a glass of lemonade, Kimmie?"

Kimmie did, and Peter poured the drinks.

"It's still a little weird to me that we are related," Kimmie admitted and sat beside Sunny. "My extended family always belonged to Dad's side."

Sunny patted her hand. "Where is Sisley?"

"I think she's in town, getting a last-minute burp cloth or something like that."

Sisley had unexpectedly arrived in Bay Harbor a month ago. Lars, Sisley's ex, had demanded she keep the pregnancy secret. Shame-faced and with all the disbelief of perfect hindsight, Sisley had admitted that his threats had scared her into compliance—until Lars, unable to deny reality any longer, decided to return to his native Norway for a fresh start. Without the baby.

"I wish Sisley had told me. I would've gotten her away from Lars," Mela had confided in Peter one night when she couldn't sleep.

"She didn't know what was happening until she was in too deep. Give her time. She'll be all right now that she has you and Kimmie." Peter kissed her shoulder, and Mela rolled to the side so she could see him in the light of the moon.

"Can she count on you too?" she asked, sleepily tracing the planes of his face with a finger.

"I'm here if she needs me," he promised. "All of us are. Sunny's obviously over the moon to have the girls. And just wait until Amelie hears the story. You'll see."

Amelie was a therapist. Mela knew her friend had heard enough heartbreaking stories to make her a fierce force against domestic abuse.

"At least Lars left on his own," she said after a while. "I hope he stays away."

The arm under Mela's head hardened into steel. "He's certainly given up all rights to the baby." Peter's voice was harsh. He liked kids, he liked Sisley, and Mela knew Lars would be wise never to come to Bay Harbor.

"He will," she said, feeling a little better.

Now, a month after she arrived, Sisley seemed to be waking from a dark dream. Every day she looked brighter and happier. Amelie had referred her to a therapist in Sandy Cove who wasn't too close to home for comfort, and Sisley had thrown herself head-on into healing her spirit and soul. She was determined to have her own fresh start. *With* the baby.

"Did she really say she was going to buy burp cloths?" Mela asked mildly and tasted the pie. A delicious pistachio-chocolate crust and crisp chocolate ganache perfectly complemented the citrusy filling. "Just because we already have hundreds of them. Certainly more than one baby could ever need." The baby was due soon, and Sisley's nesting had gone into overdrive.

Kimmie shrugged. "Maybe it was something else. Onesies? But she has hundreds of those as well."

"I don't like when Sisley's out on her own." Mela put her fork down. "Maybe you should have gone with her?"

"She didn't want company, and she's got her phone," Kimmie said reasonably. "Plus, the hospital is literally two steps away wherever she goes. Sisley knows how to get herself there if need be. This one, on the other hand"—Kimmie gave Sunny, who'd been listening interestedly, a winning smile—"refuses to use even a crutch and *does* need a helping hand. So I stayed."

"Sunny," Mela said, exasperated. "You need to build up strength in your arms. Why don't you use one of the walking aids?"

"I don't like them," Sunny said matter-of-factly. "They don't help much."

"They're temporary, and you will need them after the surgery. Better get used to them now."

Mela had taken Sunny to a doctor, and he had recommended hip surgery. They also figured out Medicare and Medicaid benefits, just to find there was no reachable doctor who accepted the plans. The tiny hospital in Bay Harbor, a remnant of the town's better days, was too small for the surgery. Fed up, Mela had finally called the university hospital in Bay Port and arranged to pay for the surgery herself.

Now, the biggest problem was Sunny herself. Mela had discovered that Sunny was scared of the surgery, boycotting progress in subtle ways. The doctor had said Sunny should build up strength in her arms. He'd also said she needed to lose weight.

Though admittedly it was hard when Amelie kept bringing them cakes and croissants and roasts with crème sauces.

"I don't want to get used to crutches."

"I should call the doctor," Mela said lightly. "Check in."

Sunny looked up, her fork guiltily suspended midair. "Later. When I'm ready."

Mela smiled. "You are ready, dear aunt. We have to schedule the surgery if we can."

"No. Yes. Oh." Sunny put her fork down and sighed deeply. "I'm not ready. I simply can't lose this stubborn weight."

"You've lost plenty. It's time to get you back to the beach."

CHAPTER 3

The young real estate agent waved Amelie to come. "Over here is the kitchen. Trust me, you'll want to have a look at this." Pride swung in her voice as if she was showing her own house.

Amelie cast a last look around the living room. It had a beautiful high ceiling, seafoam-green walls with white trim, and tall glass doors framing the sea. Stunning.

"Let's see the kitchen then," she said and followed Kelly. The kitchen was important because she really liked to... She liked to...

"Right?" Kelly said happily. "It's the best."

Amelie walked into the spacious, sparkling clean room and put a hand on the gleaming wood of the kitchen island. "It is," she managed to get out. "Oh, wow."

The kitchen was a dream. It was *her* dream. It was an amalgamate of all the kitchens in every Town & Country magazine she'd ever drooled over.

Amelie let her gaze wander over the handsome cabinets, the elegantly paneled fridge, the new stove ready to serve a crowd, the large windows with sills begging for flowers.

"It has everything." Kelly busily opened drawers and doors as if she was searching for cookies. "The cabinets and the marble here are from an old Parisian bakery, but you have all the newest appliances. The owners redid everything to their liking before they decided to sell after all."

"Goodness."

"I know. They're insanely rich," Kelly confided. "Her family wanted her to return to Singapore, so they decided to part with a few of their vacation homes."

"Well, I would never part with *this*." Images poured into Amelie's mind. Herself at the counter, making cookies. Opening the fridge, looking for butter. Cooking dinner for her friends, who were scattered around, laughing and chatting. Mela, sitting at the island, sipping wine while Amelie dried late-dinner dishes.

She turned her head. "Ooh, look!" She'd spotted a gorgeous gas fireplace with a bookshelf for cookbooks on top. "It'd be so cozy baking here in the winter. Or, you know. In the summer." Amelie folded her hands in front of her so she wouldn't start touching everything like a four-year-old. She wanted this kitchen. Badly.

"You can't find this quality, Amelie. Not in any of the houses I've sold." Kelly cleared her throat delicately.

Amelie sighed. "It's the right mix of old and new. I'm practically dying over here."

"I know," Kelly said. "And with you coming from a long line of professional bakers too."

"Yes." Amelie turned away. She wished her father had cared more about his legacy. Maybe then, buying a house like this would be as easy as snapping her fingers.

Kelly nodded, satisfied that she'd done her job. "The doors over here lead out into the sun porch, and then there's the backyard." She went to the French doors and opened them, showing the way to the prettiest little sunporch Amelie had ever seen. It had netting to keep mosquitoes out. Two sides looked out on the garden and the sea, and the third was covered by a huge butterfly bush.

Amelie immediately saw her son, Bennett, sitting in the soft green afternoon light, reading his newspaper and sipping his tea. "I love the soft light filtering through the bush," she said. "Kelly, this house is perfect."

"Do you like the garden?" Kelly pointed.

"I do like the garden." It was small for the house, but the landscaping was gorgeous. And, as far as Amelie could judge, mostly maintenance free. Best of all, it bordered a tiny, tucked-away beach that sloped down to the sea.

"You don't have to spend a lot of time gardening if you don't want to," Kelly echoed her thoughts. "The owners said to let you know about that." She paused thoughtfully. "It'll leave you more time to bake."

Amelie laughed. "Kelly, you can stop trying to convince me. I'm head over heels."

Kelly beamed at her. "Really? I'm so glad. Sometimes I show a house, and the viewers don't appreciate how perfect it is for them. Or they think I'm laying it on thick to make a quick sale. But this is the real deal, Amelie." She pulled the strap of her purse higher. "Listen—this one's not going to last. I know it's a buyer's market, but someone from Boston or New York or Singapore is going to see the online pictures and snatch it up for their Airbnb collection." She took a deep breath. "But you belong in Bay Harbor, and it has your name written all over it. I want *you* to have it."

Amelie reached for the young woman's hand. Kelly's mom, who'd been stricken with multiple sclerosis, had been a client of hers. Therapy had improved her quality of life, and her daughter was grateful. Even years later, Kelly was delighted to help when Amelie asked about the local housing market.

"Then the only problem is," Amelie said, stepping back inside, "I have to sell my house in order to buy this one."

Kelly looked crestfallen. "Amelie, I don't know—your house is nice, but it's not beachfront. We can put it on the market, but..."

Amelie sighed. "I know. I should've done that a year or two before looking. Only, I didn't know I'd want to look."

It was Mela's return to Bay Harbor that started it. All that thinking about the past, and mothers, and seeing Mela take charge to make the most of the life she still had ahead of her—it had gotten Amelie going too.

She had never planned to stay in her parents' house. In fact, she'd not planned at all. When Mom had left for Florida, Amelie had simply stayed on in the old family house. Now, watching her friend start over made Amelie want to take charge too.

"Um..." Kelly chewed her lip. "Can you maybe get a loan to bridge the time until you sell? Or ask relatives, or..." She gave up. "It's just, it won't last."

"I understand. Unfortunately, I can't do any of those things." Mom had barely enough to pay for her tasteful but tiny condo in an adult living community. "I don't have much to fall back on, Kelly." Amelie straightened. "How long do I have to put in an offer, do you think?"

Kelly frowned an apology. "Maybe I can hold out a week or two. But then they'll want the house listed, and I'll have to start showing it for real." She gripped her clipboard tighter. "Even before—if another agent asks the owners to show the house and they say yes... It could be gone in a second."

"So a second to two weeks?" Amelie shook her head. She shouldn't have started to look before she was ready to buy. "Buying a house when you own a house is such a catch twenty-two. I don't want to sell before I buy, and I can't buy before I sell."

"You're not the first one in this situation. It can be done." Kelly took a breath, slowly released it again, and smiled bravely. "What should we do? Do you still want to see the master bedroom?"

Amelie closed her eyes. "I do. I shouldn't. But I do want to see it."

"It's probably better to leave if you really don't mean to go forward. You don't want to fall in love."

It was too late for that, so Amelie had a look anyway. The bedroom—yet another fireplace—had beautifully arched windows looking out at the sea, a reading nook so cozy and inviting it almost made Amelie tear up, and a modern spa-like bathroom.

"Okay. Fine." Amelie shook her short curls. "I'm going to talk to the bank. I want this house. This is my house."

Kelly nodded, but the glance she gave Amelie was now more guarded than enthusiastic. "It's an opportunity, but there will be others. No need to break your heart over a house."

Amelie looked back at the reading nook. Talk about breaking hearts... She turned to Kelly. "Does it have a perfect room for a perfect nursery for my perfect future grandchildren?"

"It does," Kelly whispered conspiratorially. "And it has the perfect office for you too, in the little guest house out back. Private, with climbing roses in front of the windows...and a small guest apartment upstairs. It has its own kitchen aisle. You know, for visitors."

"I'll go straight to the bank," Amelie promised. Instantly, her fingertips prickled and her blood pressure rose, making it harder to breathe.

Michael Wallace, the director of the Bay Harbor Credit Union, hated Amelie as much as Kelly loved her. Evoking strong emotions in neighbors was one of the risks of being a therapist in a town where everyone knew everyone else.

"Good luck," Kelly said. "I hope he's going to behave himself." Of course she knew about Wallace.

"Well...I expect he will," Amelie said diplomatically. But she doubted he would. "I guess I'll just have to see what happens."

CHAPTER 4

Amelie drove straight from the house to the bank. All she could think about was how perfect the new house would be. Only the size was something to think about. Unless Bennett was visiting, Amelie could do with less space. But the hope was that Bennett would soon marry and have children. A lot of children. By the time Amelie pulled into the bank's four-space parking lot, her hands were sweating.

She was halfway to the door when she remembered she needed a guest room for her mother, though Meredith rarely visited. She claimed she'd moved to sunny Florida to escape the cold winters. But really, Amelie thought, it was the memory of the collapsed family empire she was avoiding.

"Amelie?" Teresa, one of two tellers, waved her over. She was a cheerful, well-rounded lady in her mid-fifties, who'd been friendly with Amelie in school even though they were in different grades. "What brings you here?"

Amelie put her purse on the counter. "Hi, Teresa. I need a loan."

"Oh." Teresa looked over her shoulder. "Do you want to talk to Michael?"

"Well—I suppose so. Unless I can talk with you?"

"I'm sorry." Teresa's big eyes widened. "You'll have to talk with him, and, um... Let me see if he's available." She threw Amelie another worried look, and then she disappeared through a door into the bank's inner sanctum.

Amelie sat on a black plastic chair, nodding at the old man, Bill Hannigan, who was already waiting there. "How are you, Bill?" she asked and smiled through her nerves. She liked the man. After retiring from his job as a police officer, Bill married Hanna, the widow who ran the local bakery and always picked the biggest bagels for Amelie. Like all cops in Bay Harbor, Bill knew about Michael's beef with Amelie.

He leaned closer, smelling of apple turnovers and sourdough bread. "Why don't you open an account with a proper bank, my dear? One of the big, anonymous ones. So you don't have to deal with him." He nodded his head at the sanctum.

"I should. Only I can't seem to get over myself. It's like I have a block."

"Why?"

"I don't know." Amelie shrugged helplessly. "Maybe because of Dad."

"Ah." Satisfied with the explanation, Bill leaned back and crossed his arms. "Too bad what happened there."

"I like the thought of a bank that works with the community. A bank where everyone knows everyone else," Amelie hurried on. She didn't want to talk about Dad.

"We all do," Bill replied, humoring her. "But it causes more problems for some than others." He coughed. "I do have another bank," he whispered and winked. "Young Wallace isn't sweet on me either."

"Probably not," Amelie confirmed.

"You did the right thing." Bill Hannigan shook his head. "Michael needs to let it go."

"Hmm." Amelie agreed but left it at that. The town already knew too much about her personal business, and sweet old Bill was a bit of a gossip.

The spare teller called Bill to the counter. He stood and patted her shoulder consolingly. "I'm convinced Kevin's proud of you." He winked, and then he left.

"Oh, goodness," Amelie whispered to herself and shifted in her hard seat.

Years ago, Amelie had been Kevin's therapist.

Like Bill, Kevin Wallace was a retired cop. He was also Michael's dad, and after the sudden death of his beloved wife, he'd been dealing with a bout of depression. Kevin's depression had been neither severe nor unsurmountable, and with Amelie's help, he made large strides towards recovery.

In fact, he made such large strides that he told Amelie he wanted a new beginning. A fresh start in a new place and gentler climate where he could reinvent himself. After faithfully serving his family, community, and nation, he felt he had earned the right to put himself first in his remaining years.

One day, when Amelie was in Florida visiting her mother, Kevin left Bay Harbor. His house was empty, and there was no note, no phone message, no trace of him.

When Amelie first heard the news, she was shocked Kevin had chosen such a hard break. But as an adult without dependents, he was allowed to disappear if he wanted. When asked, Amelie told the police her opinion: Kevin was neither a danger to himself nor anyone else.

The interview leaked to Michael and raised his hackles.

In his opinion, she'd failed his dad as a therapist and as a human being. She knew what had happened. And she lied at Michael's expense.

In short, Amelie was the source of Michael's misery.

She looked at her phone. It was taking Teresa a long time to convince Michael he had to see her...

Amelie knew that for a perfectionist like Michael, it was easier to blame her than face the difficult fact his dad hadn't included him in his new life.

After calling Amelie and sharing his exact thoughts about her qualifications as a therapist, Michael had filed a missing person report. The police calmly pointed out the missing suitcases, passport, and properly canceled utilities. They didn't do much else.

Amelie suspected *they* knew where Kevin was. But they were Kevin's friends. Even if they weren't...as far as she knew, they were legally not allowed to give his location away.

Once he understood there was no use raging against the police, Michael doubled down on his anger at Amelie. And he did more than deny credit. He'd cost her clients. Clients she couldn't afford to lose.

Suddenly, Michael appeared in the inner sanctum door, his suit pressed, his face a mask of stone. Teresa peeped over his shoulder, shrugging that she'd tried her best to soften him up.

Amelie stood. "Hi, Michael."

"Miss Cobb," Michael said. He looked up as if he hoped for divine intervention. Amelie looked too, but there was only the popcorn ceiling.

He sighed audibly and held the door open. "This way, please."

"Okay," Amelie whispered to herself. Gripping her purse like the feeble, middle-aged lady she knew he wished she was, she hurried into his office.

"Sit." He pointed to a plastic chair, taking the comfy chair behind the desk and folding his hands on the polished tabletop.

Amelie bit the inside corner of her lips. Kevin had told her many stories about Michael. Inside the angry shell was a little boy who was scared and confused because his Dad had left him. She didn't like what he was doing, but she tried to feel compassion for him and his misguided coping strategies.

"Do I have something on my face?" he asked, flushing a delicate mauve.

"No. I'm glad you have a moment for me." Amelie took a deep breath and then forged ahead, telling him about her wish to buy a new house and whether she could take out a loan to tie her over until the old house was sold and the down payment recovered.

Michael listened without looking. Then he tapped on his computer much longer than seemed necessary.

No, it turned out to nobody's surprise, she could not.

Amelie leaned forward. "Michael, I'm good for it. You know I am."

Michael leaned forward as well. "No, Amelie, you are not good for it. I don't know why you think you are. Your house is worth half what you say, you're aging out of your productive time, and your business is failing." He leaned back. "You, Amelie, don't even have enough credit at this institution to buy a decent car."

Amelie took two seconds. "Michael, how dare you?" she finally said. "You are being ageist. My business is definitely not failing."

"Well, the numbers beg to differ," he said. "Less and less income every year. I mean, I'm not surprised, but...I cannot risk loaning you money."

Amelie narrowed her eyes. "Every business experiences fluctuations. It's not that bad."

Michael's nostrils flared impatiently. "Anything else I can help you with?"

"It's not my fault that your dad decided to leave. I have literally nothing to do with it. Do you understand? You'd work with anyone else in this situation. You're being unfair."

Michael's flushed cheeks drained of color, and he stood. "I don't think you of all people can accuse me of being unfair. If a loan is all you came for, you know where the Bay Harbor Credit Union stands. If you would please leave. I have an important appointment."

Amelie rose as well. "Michael, see a therapist. Honestly. You need to talk to someone." She left the room, shook her head to answer Teresa's inquiring glance, and let herself out. Behind the building, she heard a door slam shut and then the motor of a Porsche revving. Amelie figured it was a Porsche because that's what Michael drove.

"Ugh," she muttered as she crossed the parking lot. "He's getting worse every year." She sat in her car and pulled out her phone to glance at the messages.

One was from Mela, asking if she wanted to join in making honey. One was from Meredith. Amelie groaned and swiped it away to read later.

The last one was from a client she hadn't seen in a couple of weeks. She tapped on it.

It was not Carla herself who had written from her phone, but the husband. He wanted Amelie to know that his Carla passed away a few nights ago. It had been both peaceful and expected. He thanked Amelie for her services and let her know they were no longer needed.

Amelie let her phone sink, stunned. She loved Carla. Or...she had loved Carla. Carla had come to her to talk about the great transition she was facing.

Despite her failing health, the old lady brought gratitude and joy to their sessions. It had unfailingly lifted Amelie's spirit. Carla also always brought cookies for

Bennett. She'd been his math teacher in school, and she'd adored him.

A tear fell on the phone screen, and Amelie rubbed it dry on her jeans.

She was going to *miss* Carla.

But she would think about that when she had time and space. Right now, in the hot car and under the weight of crushed expectations, Amelie couldn't face grieving her old friend.

Amelie firmly pressed the palm of her hand on her eyes, and then she started the engine. Michael's penetrating stare had lodged itself in her heart like a barbed hook, and his words started a drumbeat in her head.

Failing business.

Failing business.

Failing...failing...

Another text pinged Amelie's phone. It was from Kelly.

"New party scheduled to view house," the real estate agent texted. "U have news 4 me?"

Amelie shook her head. Her thumb accidentally hit Meredith's message, and it opened. Unlike Mom's usual style, there were only a few words. "I'm coming to Bay Harbor. Next week. Talk soon."

"What? No!" Amelie tossed the phone on the passenger seat and leaned her forehead on the steering wheel. Then she sighed, straightened back up, and pulled out of the parking spot.

First things first.

She needed to get home and call Mom.

Right now was not a good time for a visit.

CHAPTER 5

Kimmie signed the document and pushed it back to her real estate agent. Bright midmorning sunshine flooded through the window of the tiny office, and she couldn't wait to get outside. She'd never been a patient person, and the days in Bay Harbor were much too nice to waste inside. "Is that all?" she asked.

Ian looked amused. "Yes, that's all. Congratulations, Kimmie! The house is all yours. At least on paper, but the keys are coming soon." He sorted the documents into piles and glanced at her. "Are you excited?"

Was Kimmie excited about the cute yellow house waiting for her on Seasweet Lane? She jumped up. "I wish I could get in right away!"

"Just a couple more days, and you can move in. It really fell into place for you—the deal went through on the fast track. Here, these are your copies." He handed Kimmie a folder, and Kimmie stowed it in her backpack. "Are you going to celebrate?"

"I'll do that when I have the keys," Kimmie said. "Though I might go have an ice cream."

"Make it a double scoop," Ian advised and walked Kimmie to the door. "See you soon!"

Kimmie gave the agent a spontaneous hug that made the young man blush, and then she stepped into the sunshine and a future that now included her very own house by the sea.

Her stride felt twice as wide as she walked down the street toward the harbor. It was only eleven, but the soft-serve stand would be open. She planned on buying herself the biggest, swirliest ice cream with the most sprinkles.

Passing Bay Harbor's small home goods store, Maison de Mer, she spotted a familiar shape in the window. Bursting with her news, Kimmie went into the store. "Hey, Sisley, buying more stuff?"

Her little sister swung her pregnant belly around, hands full of tea towels. She looked so guilty Kimmie laughed. "What do you need tea towels for?" she asked and picked one up. It had robins on it.

"I was going to get something for Mom." Sisley sounded short of breath. She was nearly due, and Kimmie's unborn niece didn't have much consideration for her mother's lungs.

"Tea towels?"

"Well, what?" Sisley put the towels back. "I can't think of anything. She's already got all the gardening and bee stuff she could ever— Oh. Maybe this? It's so cute." She picked up a honey pot in the shape of a beehive.

"Sure," Kimmie said generously. "She'll love it."

"Hello and good morning," a deep voice came from behind her. Sisley looked up, and Kimmie turned to see.

"Bennett!" she said, beaming up at him. Bennett was Amelie's son and a detective in Cape Bass. "I didn't know you were visiting!"

They hadn't seen each other in a while, but Kimmie enjoyed hanging out with Bennett. There was something so calm and certain about him; his energy felt like the antidote to her restlessness.

"Only for the day," he said and shook first Kimmie's, then Sisley's hand. "But longer soon, I hope."

"Hi, Bennett." Sisley returned her attention to her honey pot. She'd met Bennett only once, the day she arrived. "I'll go pay for this, Kimmie." She nodded at them and went to the register. She started to chat with the store owner, who, Kimmie had learned recently, owned another store in nearby Beach Cove.

"So," Kimmie said and returned her gaze to Bennett. "What are you up to these days?"

He smiled. "Nothing much, I'm afraid."

"Yeah?" Kimmie tilted her head. "I followed a rather big case in the news. I'm fairly sure it was you who worked it."

He grinned. "Busted. But that's over. I'm taking a vacation to have a look around Bay Harbor."

"Are you still planning to move here?" Kimmie could feel excitement warm her. "I just bought a house too!" she burst out.

"Congratulations. That's marvelous. Where is it?"

"It's on Seasweet Lane," Kimmie reported. "Only a couple houses down from my mother's."

"Not too close for comfort?" He winked.

She laughed. If only Bennett knew how she felt reporting on war and devastation—it felt so good to be close to her family. "I still have my place in New York," Kimmie said. "And I still travel for my job. I'll mostly be here in the summers. But burnout was coming for me, and spending any time in Bay Harbor makes it better."

Sisley returned, holding a cute paper bag with a ribbon tying the handles together. "All done," she said happily. "Now what?"

"I just signed the papers for the house," Kimmie said. "And I would love to celebrate by buying you two an ice cream. There's a stand by the marina. What do you say?"

"Congratulation and yes, please, Kimmie. I'm hungry," Sisley said and sighed. "I'm always hungry. I can't wait to get back to normal!"

Kimmie looked at Bennett. "Do you have time?"

He cast a look around the place. The tables and shelves and racks were full of kitchen knickknacks and whimsical fabrics, homemade soaps, and local jewelry. "I was going to buy my mother a little something," he said. "But I can't think in here. There's so much stuff." He picked up a saltshaker in the form of an anchor. "I mean, what is this?"

Kimmie took the anchor from him. "It's kitsch; that's what it is," she decided. "Kitsch is in right now. Does Amelie like mermaids?"

He shrugged, looking so helpless she wanted to hug him. "No?" he guessed. "I don't think she's into that sort of thing."

"Then what does she like?" Sisley asked.

Bennett looked down as if seeing her for the first time. Kimmie almost expected him to raise his eyebrows in surprise.

"Well," he said after a moment. "She doesn't collect anything like rosters or frogs or...I don't know. Whales."

"No whales?" Sisley smiled.

"I don't think so." He ran a hand through his dark hair.

"How about this?" Kimmie picked up a rose-shaped candle from the shelf beside her. "It smells good."

Bennett took the candle. "Sure."

"Oh, look at this one." Sisley picked up another candle, this one shaped like a lily. "I love this one; it's so pretty. Get her this one too; they go together. Same color, different shapes."

"Okay." Bennett took it from her, holding the delicate candles in his big hands. "You ladies go ahead down to the marina. It'll take me a minute to pay."

"You'll catch up with us in no time." Sisley smiled weakly. "I'm embarrassed to say this, but I can barely waddle anymore. I think all my bones have melted."

Kimmie took her sister's arm. She wasn't a hugger, but this was different. Sisley really could barely walk anymore. Bennett didn't need to know all the gory details, but the doctor had said Sisley's pelvic bones were starting to separate. Walking had become painful, but Sisley wasn't going to let it stop her.

"We'll take the head start," Kimmie said. Sisley gave her a grateful look and leaned on her arm as they made their way to the exit.

They'd never been close. At home, there'd been great schools, expensive after-school activities, the latest toys. It was all right when they were little. Then, during their teen years, the family had often been short on time to spend together. Kimmie, Sisley, and their brother Morris drifted apart. Getting a grateful look from Sis was new—and nice.

"I'm glad you came to Bay Harbor," Kimmie said when she pushed open the door. "I've seen you maybe a dozen times since you turned fifteen."

Sisley nodded. Already she was breathing hard with effort. "I'm not sure I would recognize Morris if I met him on the street."

Kimmie chuckled at the exaggeration. "Of course you would. I hope he'll come visit Mom sometime soon."

"I know." Sisley shook her head, slowly making her way toward the small marina, where locals kept their sailboats and rowboats. The big fishing vessels were moored in the harbor. "I'm worried he is as much of a mess as me."

"Well," Kimmie said. "He *is* a bit different."

"He's different," Sisley agreed. "But don't tell Mom. She thinks he's a genius."

Mom had worked the hardest to straighten Morris out. It'd gotten better when he grew older and learned to channel his gifts, but he'd moved out before turning nineteen. The family had rarely seen him since. Who knew what he was up to, Kimmie thought.

"All done," Bennett's voice sounded behind them. Kimmie stopped, and they turned.

"May I?" Bennett stepped between them, offering an arm to each.

Kimmie let go of her sister and took Bennett's left arm while Sisley did the same on his right side. Kimmie smiled at him, and he smiled back.

"Lucky me," he said. "To have two beautiful friends to take out for ice cream."

"*I'm* the one taking you out," Kimmie insisted. "I started the ice cream thing."

"No dice," Bennett replied contentedly, slowing his pace to their speed. "I will wither and die if you don't let me pay, and I know you're too kind to let that happen." He looked at Sisley. "Am I going too fast? Are you comfortable?"

Sisley laughed. "I'm not going to be comfortable again until this baby is born."

Bennett slowed down a little more, and Kimmie sighed. "Well," she said, resigned to a snail's pace, "it's still an hour or two to the marina. How about a story, Bennett? Tell us how you caught that guy."

He shook his head. "I can't, but I can tell you about another case. This one was five years ago, and I was still green behind the ears."

He launched into a story that was more funny than fierce, and soon, he had both Kimmie and Sisley laughing.

CHAPTER 6

By the time they reached the marina, the sun was glaring on cobblestones and water. The water, bright and blue, glared right back. Kimmie wiped her forehead. The temperature was already at swimsuit degrees with a chance of beach towel.

Bennett steered them to a shady bench, quizzed them about their ice cream preferences, and went to order them.

"He's really nice," Sisley said, watching his tall form stride across the parking lot.

Kimmie nodded. "He is."

She wondered how Sisley was doing in the love department. Lars, her ex, abruptly decided not to take part in the baby's life. From what little Sisley had shared, the relationship had been at least emotionally abusive. Maybe worse.

Sisley leaned back and closed her eyes, both hands resting on her belly. There was a sheen of sweat on her forehead. "I can feel you worrying about me, Kimmie. I'm all right now. You know—" She opened one eye.

"What?"

"I feel terrible saying this, but it was lucky for me that Mom and Dad divorced."

"Oh. Well, I never thought of it as *lucky*." Kimmie knew divorce had been the right thing for her parents. But it was sad. So many years and so much history together and then...bam. All gone.

"I'm not sure I would have come to Dad," Sis admitted. "I was too embarrassed. There I was, unmarried and pregnant and not even a college degree to show for all my choices. I always wanted to be perfect for him."

Kimmie pressed her lips into a line. "Me too." She was still trying. After every assignment, she called Dad to tell him about it, thinking he would be impressed. Maybe he was—only, he never said so.

"But with Mom, you can just be the way you are," Sisley said. "With her, you get to be good enough."

"Of course you're good enough. But I know what you mean."

Guiltily, Kimmie shifted her weight. Sisley had always seemed a little aimless to her, picking up this and that hobby and dropping it again. Kimmie had followed her interests with laser-like precision. Only since coming to Bay Harbor had she figured out that there was a cost to her focus. Experimenting and expanding, discovering new interests, finding love.

Kimmie's thoughts whipped to Travis. The man she had married in good faith. The man who had divorced her before she turned thirty.

"Here you go," Bennett said. He was balancing three soft-serve ice creams that twisted their creamy chocolate-strawberry-vanilla way higher than they had any right to be.

"Oh my goodness." Kimmie jumped up to help him. "How did you get them to make them so big?"

"It's my devastating charm," Bennett said distractedly, wiping a dribble of cream off his hand with a napkin.

"I bet." Kimmie handed a cone to her sister and sat back down. She tasted the twisted tip of her ice cream. "It's—"

"Unbelievable," Sisley said with a little sigh. "This is the best thing I've ever eaten in my entire life." She patted the seat between herself and Kimmie. "Come, Bennett, sit with us. Thank you very much for the ice cream. It hits the spot."

Bennett sat, and for a while they ate in comfortable silence, trying to beat the heat that melted the ice cream.

"Bennett," Kimmie said when she had licked her mountain into shape so it would run into the cone instead of her hand. "You never said whether you were thinking about moving here."

"Ah." He had already reached the cone and bit into it. "Yes. I've applied for a job here because I want to be near my mother. She doesn't have any other family. I figured I'd move sooner rather than later."

"What about your dad?" Sisley inspected her ice cream.

"Not in the picture," Bennett said curtly.

Kimmie looked up. She'd not heard him sound like this before.

"Your house," he said and turned to her. "Tell us about it. I might look at the market myself. I'm not sure I want to buy, though."

"It's small but pretty." Kimmie finished her cone and wiped her hands. "You've seen it driving to Mom's house. It has three bedrooms upstairs, and downstairs are a living room, family room, and kitchen. It has access to the beach, but the property is a little crooked, so it's not as nice as Mom's."

"It doesn't have to be," Sisley said. "I'm so proud of you to be able to buy a house just like that, Kimmie. Well done."

"Thank you. I'm a little proud myself."

Sisley leaned forward so she could see around Bennett. "You're my shining star, you know," she said. "I've always looked up to you."

"Aww...Sisley, I had no idea." Kimmie felt her cheeks flush with pleasure. Bennett smiled at her, and she flushed even more.

"You always knew what you wanted and how to get it." Sisley leaned back. "I've never felt like that. Well, no. When I found out about this"—she patted her belly—"I knew I wanted her. It was a huge shock. *Huge*. But I knew right away I wanted her. It's how I imagine you feel about...well, everything you do."

Kimmie shook her head, but she didn't say anything. Because that's not how any of it felt. There was so much love and contentment in Sisley's voice when she said she'd known right away.

For Kimmie, reporting what the world couldn't see but needed to know was a burden. It was *her* burden, something she needed to shoulder because she *could*, but she felt no love and contentment. Only duty and drive.

Again, her thoughts went to Travis. One day, she came back from a project and he'd left the divorce papers on her nightstand.

It had been the end of her dream that life could be more. Something warmer, more giving and nurturing. She'd thrown herself back into work, and by the time Dad sent her to Bay Harbor, the shell she'd been cementing around herself had been almost complete.

But it was impossible to be in a sweet seaside town and not tear down the wall a little to better see the pink hydrangeas and taste the fresh blueberries and feel the cold waves tickle your bare feet. Bare feet, bare soul—in Bay Harbor, healing was possible.

"Are you all right?" Bennett looked at her, the slightest frown on his face. "We can leave if you want to."

Kimmie shook her head, surprised to find that she was near crying because her chaotic little sister had paid her a compliment. "I'm all right," she said quietly so her voice wouldn't waver. "Everything is perfect."

Sisley announced she had to use the bathroom and they were to wait for her. She hobbled off, refusing any help, leaving Kimmie and Bennett alone.

Suddenly, Kimmie wanted nothing more than to rest her head on Bennett's shoulder. But even though she and Bennett had casually flirted when they first met, it felt too bold.

"I'm glad you're okay," he said. "For a moment there, I thought you were crying."

"I never cry," Kimmie said. "But thank you."

"So..." He took a breath that expanded his chest and looked out at the ocean. Sunbeams were skipping over the surface, changing the water from turquoise to sapphire and back. "I hope this isn't too forward... My mom said you were married?"

Kimmie glanced at him from the corner of her eye. "It didn't work out."

He nodded. "Is he still around?"

"No." She had no idea where Travis was. He was a reporter like her, forever traveling. The urge to rest on Bennett's shoulder, which was safe and right *there* became overwhelming. Kimmie tried not to lean.

Suddenly, Bennett took her hand. "I have pretty good intuition, Kimmie," he said gently. "Detectives tend to develop that skill. And my intuition tells me that whatever happened with your marriage, you aren't in the clear yet." He waited until she met his eyes. "Of course I could be wrong. It's happened before." He smiled, but his eyes were guarded. "What does your own intuition say?"

Chapter 7

Driftwood Dairy had the best public restroom in town—clean, cool, full towel dispenser, spacious enough even for a pregnant lady.

Sisley took her time washing her hands and raking her long blond hair back. Of course she should've thought of an excuse when the ice-cream plan was first made. It simply hadn't occurred to her that Kimmie was divorced and might like time alone with Bennett.

Sisley felt like a third wheel. But when there was nothing left to do and she couldn't justify occupying the restroom any longer, she made her way back. It looked as if Kimmie and Bennett were deep in conversation, and then Bennett took Kimmie's hand into his own.

Sisley stopped.

No way was she going to barge in on that one.

Now Kimmie was looking deep into Bennett's eyes. Sisley turned around.

She'd rather waddle all the way back to Seasweet Lane than interrupt. She could do it, too, even though the baby was pressing down hard, and her pelvis burned from all the walking she'd already done. Every couple of steps she would just take a break and—

Wet ran down her leg, trickling onto the warm asphalt. Sisley stopped, mortified. She'd just gone to the bathroom a second ago! Suddenly, the skirt of her maternity dress stuck to her leg, clingy and hot. Sisley felt her eyes widen with shock. It couldn't be true, could it? She still had a couple of weeks! Maybe a leak? Had she drunk too much water?

But no—no, this was it. The countdown was on.

Sisley gulped a lungful of air. Her hands shook with nerves. "Kimmie?" she called out. "Kimmie?"

"Sisley!"

Sisley looked over her shoulder. She was frozen to the spot. "I need you," she mouthed. Kimmie jumped up and ran toward her, Bennett a close second.

Sisley squeezed her eyes shut. Through the haze in her mind pressed the thought, why in public? Why now?

She took a step, but the burning pressure on her pelvis was too much. She winced, and then Kimmie grabbed her arm. "Let's get you to the hospital, Sis. Your water broke."

Sisley nodded, but even though Kimmie was strong, her grip wasn't enough support. "I can't walk," Sisley whimpered. This was scary. This wasn't how the nurse had described it. There was no timing of contractions and calling the hospital to check in.

"I'm parked close by." Bennett's voice was calm. "You're all right, Sisley. You're doing great. Don't be scared."

"I'm..." Her belly cramped. Sisley hissed out what breath was left in her, and Kimmie grabbed her arm so hard it hurt.

"Right." Bennett strode off.

"I can't..." Suddenly, her lungs worked again, and Sisley gasped.

"Don't worry about a thing, Sis," Kimmie said. "You'll be fine. The baby will be fine. It will work out great."

It fluttered through Sisley's mind that she didn't want to be in Bennett's car in her soaked skirt, soiling his seats, but then her belly cramped again, and she couldn't think of anything but the breathing technique the nurse had taught her. Two short pants followed by a long exhale. It didn't help. She tried again, her breath too loud because she was scared it wasn't all right after all.

"Oh *dear*," Kimmie said, and she sounded so nervous that Sisley suddenly felt a little better. She giggled despite the contraction.

"You go to war zones." She gulped in another breath. "This is...nothing in comparison." Pant, pant, blow.

"I don't know," Kimmie said, clearly shaken. "Maybe if you weren't my sister..."

A car pulled up. A second later, Bennett took Sisley's other arm, slung an arm around her nonexistent waist, and lifted her enough she could waddle the two steps to the car. He lifted her into the back seat, Kimmie ran around to the other side and got in beside her, doors slammed, and then Bennett pulled into the street.

"To the hospital, please," Sisley said, and then she moaned, loud and embarrassing, because another contraction hit, and this one *hurt*.

"Are they supposed to come this quick?" Kimmie asked, taking her hand.

"They're here to stay," Bennett remarked calmly from the front. "It's not going to be long before you have your baby girl in your arms, Sisley."

Sisley nodded, letting his deep voice calm her as the contraction ebbed away. "How far is it?"

"Right around the corner," Bennett said. "You're not my first rush delivery to a hospital, so relax and trust me. I'll get you there in time."

The hospital—a small, clean-cut building—was indeed close, and Bennett and Kimmie had Sisley out of the car before another contraction started.

Kimmie ran ahead inside while Sisley clung to Bennett, and a minute later, a nurse whisked her into a wheelchair and the building, handing her a bracelet to snap on.

A wave of relief washed over Sisley. She felt safer now; the air was cool and smelled of disinfectant and help at hand. She turned in her chair as much as she could, seeing Kimmie waving her cell phone—she was going to call Mom—while Bennett was talking to the lady at the registration.

The nurse was in her fifties and behaved as if giving birth was like baking a sheet of cookies: fun, easy, and the result about as predictable. She rolled Sisley into a delivery room, joking lightly, and Sisley gratefully accepted her help undressing and putting on a gown.

"You can be in the bed, or you can go on the birthing ball if you like," the nurse, explained. "Was that your husband taking care of insurance at the registration?"

"Um, no. That was a friend." Sisley hobbled onto the bed and gingerly rested against the raised back. She liked how he'd kept his cool. He didn't twitch an eyelid when she sat in his car, soaked skirt and all.

Lars would've barked at her. He always did when he was overwhelmed. Sisley breathed her way through another contraction while Lilly took her vitals and left to get fresh mattress pads.

The was a short pause during which Sisley arranged herself more comfortably on the bed, though nothing was very comfortable. The door opened again, and Mom rushed in. "Sisley, sweetheart! Are you okay?"

Sisley nodded. Another contraction was coming on, and she closed her eyes, bracing herself.

"Breathe with me," Mom said and took her hand. She modeled the rhythm, and Sisley followed her example until the cramp receded like an ebbing wave.

When she opened her eyes, Mom was smiling. "Well done," she said. "I'm so proud of you. Do you need anything?"

Sisley shook her head. "I'm glad you're here," she said. "I'm glad it's you and not Lars. I never want to see him again."

"You don't have to," Mom assured her. "You can let him know when the baby is here. But you don't have to do that, either."

"No," Sisley said. She'd meant what she'd said. "He left us hanging when we needed him most. I'll never forgive him for that."

Her mother wiped Sisley's hair from her face. "Forgive him for your own sake, or you'll always have a sore heart, darling. It doesn't mean you have to invite him back into your life."

"I certainly *won't*." Sisley grimaced in pain as another contraction tightened her belly. "It's getting worse."

The door opened, and a doctor entered, the nurse right behind her. "Well, let's see how far along we are, shall we?" the doctor said jovially and pulled on blue gloves. "I'm Dr. Haverstraw, and you already met Lilly. You are Sisley Beckett?"

Sisley could only nod.

Dr. Haverstraw and Lilly glanced at the record of her vitals while Sisley rode out the pain, and then the doctor checked her.

"Not long now," she announced cheerfully. "Let's check on the baby." She listened to the heartbeat. "You'll have a strong, healthy baby girl," she promised, and Lilly beamed at Sisley.

Two hours that both quickly rushed and slowly crawled fulfilled the doctor's promise, and finally, Lilly handed Sisley her baby daughter and stepped back. Tears trickled down her mother's face as she blotted

Sisley's forehead and pushed her hair back. "Congrat-ulations," she whispered. "You did great. I love you."

The words dissolved Sisley's shame and anger and all the ways she wished things had gone differently like salt in the rain. She and her baby would never be alone again because they had a mother and grandmother who loved them. The nurse from the birthing class had promised a rush of hormonal happiness after the birth, and Sisley felt the swelling wave of oxytocin lift her, fighting the fatigue that made it hard to keep her eyes open.

Mom went outside to talk to the doctor while Lilly showed Sisley how to nurse her daughter. After the baby fell asleep on Sisley's chest, Mom came back, smiling widely. "Kimmie asks if she can come in to see her niece," she said and tucked Sisley's cover in. "Bennett waited too, by the way. He'll stay outside."

Sisley turned her head. "No, it's okay," she said. "Bring Bennett in. Thanks to him my baby was born in a hos-pital, not a parking lot." She was too weak to say more. But she knew how grateful she was to him.

"All right," Mom said, smiling. "I'll bring him in too."

CHAPTER 8

A new nurse had rolled Sisley into a different room to spend the night. Her family and friends left, and Sisley, even though she'd napped fitfully, was tired from what had turned into a very long day. Her baby—still nameless and a tiny stranger despite the love Sisley felt for her—lay in a bassinet beside the bed.

The nurse closed the blinds. "Are you sure you want to keep her with you? She can sleep in the nursery so you can catch some rest. You did a great job, but your body needs time to recover. Once you're home, you'll be on duty for the next, oh, let's say, sixteen years? Unless Dad pitches in, of course."

Sisley looked at her baby. "I'll try to sleep tonight. Dad's not in the picture, so I can't say no when people offer help."

The nurse nodded. "I think that's a wise call. She'll be just fine with us. Do you want me to bring her in for nursing, or are you okay if she gets a bottle? I recommend the bottle, just so you can get more sleep."

"No, I'll nurse her," Sisley said, half regretting her decision not to spend this first night with her newborn.

But there were so many nights to come, and she was exhausted from giving birth. Whether she liked it or not, she had to pace herself. "Thank you for taking care of my little one."

"Of course," the nurse said, lightly touching Sisley's shoulder. "Go ahead and get some sleep. You had a good delivery and will heal quickly, but you've done enough for today." Without further ado, she rolled the bassinet out of the room.

The door to Sisley's room swung shut with a soft plop. For what seemed like the first time in weeks, she was alone.

She closed her eyes, trying to fall asleep.

After half an hour, her thoughts started to circle.

Should she call Lars?

Sisley remembered how he had come home one day and announced he was leaving. Just like that. She'd put a hand on her belly, feeling her heartbeat speed up with stress, going faster and faster. She was scared to do anything but nod. She was scared of Lars, full stop. She'd known their relationship was unhealthy, but part of her disease was that she thought she could fix it. That she could find the right words, the right way to act, the right path to his heart. She still wasn't sure what had made her try so hard.

Now, it reminded her of how she'd tried to get Dad's love and attention. As the youngest, she'd had the least access to him. He'd rarely been at her school events, and whenever Sisley tried to engage him, he would turn away to more important matters. As a little girl, she hadn't had a choice but to keep trying. Lars had simply tapped into the energy she brought to their relationship. And Sisley had allowed it.

But that was over. She would never run after a man again. She would never again beg for love. She closed her eyes and made a promise. Not only to her baby but also to the little girl that still lived inside her.

The weight that had pressed her into the shape of a coward was lifting. Clumsily, she turned on her side. For a while, she listened to the distant rushing of the sea, trying to sleep but feeling too wired despite her fatigue. She opened her eyes. There was no hope of rest until she'd settled this for good. Gingerly, Sisley sat up and fished her phone from the nightstand. Did Lars still use this number? She pressed the button, her heart fluttering. There was a dial tone, so—

"Sisley?" It was Lars's voice. Not his cold voice, but his nice one, the one that used to make her happy. "Did the baby come?"

"Hello, Lars." Sisley took a breath. She was cold. "Yes, she was born today."

There was a moment of silence. "Are you okay?"

"I'm okay. She is too."

"Good."

Sisley moistened her lips. "I wanted to let you know."

"It was your choice to have it," he said. "I didn't want to—"

"You don't have to do that anymore," she interrupted. "It's okay. I'm not asking you to be in our lives. But now there's a little girl who shares half of your genes. I thought you should know. That's it. That's all."

"So you... Do you want anything from me?"

Sisley shivered. The hospital blanket covering her legs was thin and cool, and goosebumps rose on her arms. "I want nothing from you. Just think of her with love, if you think of her at all." She pulled the blanket higher. "It's not her fault we couldn't work it out."

"I didn't do anything wrong," Lars said, sounding more subdued than righteous; a little boy, unable to admit his mistake. He cleared his throat a few times. "Well, it's kind of late here."

"It's late here too." Sisley sighed. "I'm going to delete your number from my phone now, Lars. I'm not going to get in touch again. Don't call me either."

He made a sound of relief. Her words had lifted a weight off him, too. "Hey—Sisley?"

"Yes."

"Do you have a name yet?"

"I have a shortlist."

She heard him inhale. "Put Lovise on there? It's Norwegian, and I've always liked it."

Sisley struggled for a moment. Lars didn't deserve to name their baby. Besides, she'd been thinking about Emma, or Emily, or maybe Claire... Though none of the names hit home. And Lovise was nice.

She shook her head even though Lars couldn't see her. "I don't think so, Lars. You don't get to name her."

He took a moment before he responded. "I know. But you don't have to tell her where it came from."

Something tilted in Sisley's chest. Maybe it was the oxytocin overload, maybe Mom's earlier words about forgiveness. Maybe it was the thought that giving her daughter this one gift from her father might mean something to her later. A token of acknowledgment, a nod in the direction of her existence... It was better than just being abandoned, wasn't it?

"I'm not going to ask for anything else. I promise."

Sisley didn't like Lars. But she wanted her daughter to live in a world full of forgiveness and kindness, not anger and resentment.

She never had to tell.

And Lovise really was cute.

"Okay," she said finally. "I like the name too."

"I'm not... I can't be in her life," Lars said. "You know it's better if I'm not."

"I know."

"But I'm glad Lovise is with you."

Sisley waited for a moment, but he didn't say anything else.

"Bye, Lars." Sisley ended the call, and then she deleted his number. There was no need to keep it anymore. She had nothing else to tell him.

"Lovise," Sisley said out loud, tasting the name. "Lovise Beckett. Lovie." She smiled. The name fit the newborn with her big eyes and rosebud lips.

Her thoughts were interrupted by a knock on the door.

"Yes?"

The door opened, and the nurse peeked in. "Time to nurse. Did you get some sleep?"

"Nope." Sisley smiled. Suddenly, she couldn't wait to have Lovie back. "Did you bring her?"

"Yes, you bet. She's getting cranky." The nurse rolled in the bassinet, and there was little Lovise, swaddled and with a tiny hat that made her look like a small acorn. She was the most beautiful person Sisley had ever seen, despite the puckered forehead.

The nurse picked Lovie up and handed her to Sisley, and when Sisley felt the six pounds and twelve ounces of her baby in her arms, it was like holding love itself. She swallowed before she could talk.

"I've changed my mind," she said. "I'll keep her with me now, please."

The nurse smiled. "Ah, I see," she said. "Sometimes, it goes like that. I bet you'll go home tomorrow."

"Yes," Sisley said. "Tomorrow, we'll go home."

CHAPTER 9

Mela pulled up in front of the curb and looked into her rearview mirror. Sisley was sitting behind her, a hand on the baby in the car seat. The afternoon sun was slanting through the rear window, making Sisley's honey hair shine.

She looked so much like her grandmother. Julie, too, had brought Mela home without a proud dad and even without much of a family waiting for them. Sisley had Mela and Kimmie and a whole team of found family and friends eagerly awaiting the new arrival.

"Ready?" Mela asked and smiled.

"Yes." Sisley looked up, and their eyes met.

"You've got this," Mela promised. "We're here to help."

Her daughter nodded. "I know. Thank you, Mom."

The door opened, and Kimmie came jumping down the stairs. Sunny, who'd not been able to come to the hospital the day before, limped out the door to greet the new mom and baby.

Mela got out of the car and waved.

"Well, hello there, mama," Kimmie greeted her sister and helped her out of the car while Mela unbuckled the baby seat and pulled it out. Little Lovise had been sleeping peacefully in the car, but the movement woke her. She blinked into the light and at Mela, who smiled back and tickled the chubby cheek.

Sunny grabbed Sisley, who'd walked to the door on Kimmie's arm, by the shoulders. "Look at you!" Sunny exclaimed. "Nothing left but skin and bones!"

"Yeah, I don't know about that." Sisley laughed. Her midsection had deflated, but she was still far from looking like before. But better than skinny, she was glowing with happiness. Mela hadn't seen her this happy in years.

Again, Mela's thoughts went to Julie. Mela wasn't born in Bay Harbor. But if she had been, maybe Julie would have stood in this door, looking exactly like Sisley.

"Mom? Are you coming?"

"Yes. Yes."

They all went into the living room, where Kimmie lowered Sunny onto the sofa and then held out a hand to help Sisley.

"I can sit by myself, you know," Sisley said, amused.

"I know," Kimmie said and patted her little sister's arm. "I'm just trying to be nice for a change."

Mela tilted her head. Kimmie wasn't only nicer. She had slowed down, taking time to enjoy life. Bay Harbor was good for the sisters. She set the baby carrier between Sisley and Sunny, who was already fussing over the newborn.

"I'm going to get the cake," Mela announced. "Sunny baked it this morning."

"It smells delicious." Sisley sighed happily and put her purse on the ground.

"I already tried to get a slice, but Sunny wouldn't budge." Kimmie squatted to unstrap the baby. "Hi, sweetheart," she cooed, lifting Lovie from her seat.

"Can I hold her?" Sunny held out her hands, eyes shining. "Goodness, how tiny are you? And so cute! Sisley, sweetheart, well done!"

Mela stood behind them, enjoying the sight of her family. She wanted to hold Lovie too, but she'd already had more than her fair share of baby time. She went into the kitchen and made tea, then lifted the glass dome off the cake.

"My adopted mother was German." Sunny came limping into the kitchen. Through the door, Mela saw Kimmie dancing with Lovie in her arms. "And this is the German crown cake she made for special occasions. She called it Frankfurter Kranz."

"Frankfurt like the town?"

Sunny nodded. "They used to crown the German emperor there. That's why it's a crown cake."

"What sort of cake is it?" It was covered in caramelized hazelnuts, but Mela didn't know what was below the sweet surface.

"It's a mix of a pound cake and a sponge cake," Sunny said critically. "Layered with raspberry jelly and buttercream. There are supposed to be maraschino cherries on top, but we didn't have any."

Mela laughed. "It looks like there'll be enough to eat even without the maraschino cherries." She shook her head at Sunny because Sunny was supposed to lose weight for the surgery.

"Don't worry, I made it for Sisley. I'll only have a tiny taste," Sunny said sorrowfully. "I want to get this new hip so I can take a proper walk again."

Mela heard the longing in her aunt's voice. "The sooner, the better," she agreed. "You can have cake after the surgery—though maybe we'll make something with less butter. The two of us have to look out for our waistlines."

"Not you," Sunny said mildly. "But thank you for trying to make it better."

"Here." Mela handed her a knife.

Sunny cut the cake, putting huge slices of fluffy cake on the plates, and Mela brought tea and cake into the living room.

There was a knock on the door, and Peter came in. He handed Sisley a bouquet of cornflowers and baby's breath. "Congratulations, my dear," he said and kissed her cheek. "The baby looks like a perfect...baby."

"Do you want to hold her?" Sisley handed him Lovise.

"Sure." Peter took the newborn, cradling her in his arms. Lovie stared at him, her fist moving aimlessly in the air.

Mela glanced at Sisley and saw how intently her daughter watched Peter. It made Mela ache a little—Robert called at the hospital and congratulated her, but he wasn't making time to see his grandchild until next month.

A not-so-small corner in Mela's heart wished he'd carved out a few hours for Sisley. As the youngest, she'd always gotten the short stick when it came to her father's attention.

"Let's sit," she said and helped Sunny get comfortable. Kimmie handed out plates, Mela poured the tea, and then their small crowd fell quiet because the Frankfurter crown cake was that good.

Before Mela had eaten half of her slice, little Lovie started to squirm in Peter's arm. Mela set down her plate and took the baby so he could have some cake too.

"I think she might be good for a nap. Do you want to lie down with her, Sis?" she asked after a while. Sisley, happy and blooming as she was, looked like she could use a nap herself.

"That sounds good. Kimmie, can you help me upstairs?"

"Sure." Kimmie did as her sister asked, and Mela followed with the baby.

Mela had moved into her mother Julie's bedroom. Kimmie was in Mela's childhood room, and the other two small rooms had been fixed up for Sisley's bedroom and nursery.

Sisley nursed and then washed and brushed her teeth while Mela changed Lovie's diaper. When she heard Sisley finish, Mela brought the baby to her. Sisley was lying in bed, her eyes closed. She opened them when Mela lowered the baby into the bassinet beside the bed.

"Hi, Mom," Sisley said.

"Hi, sweetheart." Mela sat on the bed. Lovie's eyes were already closing. "Do you need anything?"

"I'm good." Sisley took Mela's hand. "I'm sorry, Mom," she said. "I should be in my own house instead of yours. I'll do my best to get on my feet quickly."

"You're doing plenty already." Mela wiped her daughter's hair out of her face. "I'm in *my* mom's house, aren't I?" She smiled. "Life's not straight like that, my dear. You expect one thing and get another. It doesn't mean it's wrong. Just different."

"No, it's not wrong." Sisley smiled sleepily. "But I want to be like Kimmie. She's got a career and bought a house before turning thirty."

"Dad and I helped a little," Mela said. "And we'll help you too. You figure out what it is *you* want to do. That's the way to make it all fall into place."

"I want to stay in Bay Harbor," Sisley murmured. "I feel safe here. I feel like this is home."

Mela nodded. "That's how it has always felt to me too." She rose to close the curtains. The bright August sun of an early afternoon was streaming through the windows.

"There is time for everything," she promised. "There's no hurry."

"That's why I like Bay Harbor. There's no hurry." Sisley yawned. "Can you wake me in half an hour?"

"We'll see how Lovise does." Quietly, Mela tiptoed out of the room.

CHAPTER 10

"Are you going to the bee yard?" Peter was stacking the plates on the coffee table.

"I meant to. What happened to Kimmie and Sunny?" Mela looked around the empty living room.

"Kimmie got a call from her real estate agent and left," Peter reported.

"Is there a problem?"

"She didn't say anything, and I didn't want to pry. Sunny went to lie down for a nap, too. I think she's hurting. Look." He held up a plate with a mostly untouched piece of cake. "She's only had a taste."

Mela gathered the cups. "I can't wait for that surgery to be over. She has another doctor's appointment soon, and then we'll see if it's a thumbs-up."

"It depends on her weight?"

"Probably. She's trying to be good, only she isn't always. But I'm hoping it will be enough."

Peter carried the plates into the kitchen and set them in the sink, and Mela added her cups. "Let's leave them for later," he whispered. "I don't want to wake Sunny up."

He took her hand, and they walked outside onto the patio, where the air smelled of kelp and salt and the lavender growing by the wall. "Your house is getting full," Peter said. "I think it's time we meet at the motel more often. I'm all alone in it, and it's awfully empty."

Mela put her arms around his neck and kissed him. "I thought life here would be so slow," she said, only half-joking. "I'm almost as busy as before."

Peter waggled his eyebrows. "I should've tried harder to keep you for myself."

"They're my family," Mela said sternly. "I love you, but I also love my family."

Peter kissed her forehead. "Say that again."

"I love my family," Mela repeated and was rewarded with a squeeze that made her laugh. "I love you, Peter," she said when she could. "I'm pretty sure I've always loved you."

"I know I have," he said. "And I'm more than just *pretty* sure." He let her go. "I can spare a couple of hours if you need help with the bees."

"I don't need help, but I'd love your company," Mela said. "I want to check for Varroa mites. They can take a healthy colony down before you know it."

They gathered bee hats and tools from the barn, and Peter drove the truck out to the field, parking in the shade of an old oak.

Grass and flowers swayed gently in the breeze when they got out, and beyond the field, the sea shimmered as soft as the afternoon sky.

"This is how I remember my Bay Harbor summers," said Mela. She leaned against the truck bed and pushed her hands into the pockets of her jeans. "I thought I was being nostalgic. Is the weather always this beautiful, or is it just a particularly nice year?"

"Both." Peter picked a stem of sweet grass to put between his lips. "It's always a particularly nice summer here. We are lucky that way."

"I can't start to count the ways," Mela agreed. "The kids, the house, the place, Sunny, you..." She blinked into the sky. "I think I'm manifesting my perfect life."

"I wish I had kids," Peter said suddenly. He sounded wistful. "When I held the little one there, I felt like I missed out."

Mela knew he'd had relationships. They'd talked about it—not in too much detail, only enough to catch each other up in broad strokes.

While she'd spent most of her life married to Rob, Peter had had shorter relationships. He'd been engaged once to another scientist, but the woman cheated on him before the wedding date was set. When Peter realized he didn't care as much as he thought he should, they called off the engagement and went their separate ways.

Peter grabbed a veil. "Shall we beekeep?" he asked, clearly done talking about his regrets.

Mela nodded. "We shall," she said and turned to get her tools.

While Peter strapped on a hat and veil, she set fire to a rag and stuffed it into the smoker. Inside the closed vessel, the flame soon choked, and smoldering burlap smoke spilled from the nozzle.

They went through the knee-high grass to the closest hive. Peter puffed smoke at the entrance, and Mela pushed her hive tool in between the hive body and lid.

The bees had glued the lid to the box with wax and propolis. Mela gently pried it off and set it on the ground. She pulled out a frame, scanning the comb for the queen. "Could you give me some smoke?"

Peter blew over the bees who were nervously running over the comb, wings buzzing and behinds high in the air. "What does the smoke do to them?" he asked. "Does it choke them?"

"The smoke makes them think their tree is on fire."

"They're not in a tree."

"But they think they are."

He puffed again. "It still doesn't explain why smoke keeps them from stinging."

"Stinging doesn't do much to fire. Instead, they go drink all the honey they can. They figure they have to move out and should bring as much food as they can."

There was the queen, running just like everyone else. Mela nudged her carefully back into the hive. "But if you breathe on bees, they think a bear is doing it. They'll attack to defend their nest."

"Let's not do that, then," Peter said.

"And if you eat a banana, they attack as well," Mela added. "Because their alarm pheromone smells like banana."

"Banana. Got it." Peter grinned. "That one seems pretty random. What else?"

"Hmmm." Mela pulled out another frame. "Wearing bright colors is better than black."

"Because bears are black?"

Mela nodded and inspected another frame. "Bears and bees just don't get along. At least from the bees' point of view, I suppose."

He craned his neck. "What do you see?"

Mela frowned. "There are some mites. More than I'd like."

"What's that, mold?" He pointed at an area where the cells were orange and yellow and even green.

Mela shook her head distractedly. "That's pollen. That's what they eat." She put the frame back. "I mean, the babies. That's what the babies get to eat."

"Bad?" Peter looked at her.

"Pretty bad." Varroa mites were infamous for killing colonies. She'd brought medication, but there was work to do before she could apply it. "We'll need to take out the rest of the honey. It becomes inedible after I treat the mites. I'll also have to go through and put all the brood frames together. That's where the mites breed."

"Let's go," Peter said and puffed more smoke.

Mela smiled. "It might take a while, even if we only do half the hives today."

"I still have empty boxes and frames on the truck to swap out."

They removed the honey frames. Then Mela pulled on a pair of rubber gloves and took a medicated plastic strip from a bag, slipping it between brood frames. "I hope we caught it early enough." She wiggled the last strip in place and straightened to wipe the sweat from her brow.

"I'll close the hives," Peter offered. "Go sit in the shade."

"Thank you." Mela got a bottle of water from the icebox in the truck and sat in the shade of an alley oak, watching Peter as he lifted the last boxes back into place and put the lids back on the hives. The hot, floral air was full of bees, and the sea below the bluff looked cool and inviting. As soon as she caught her breath, Mela brought Peter a bottle of water.

"Do you want to go for a swim?" She nodded at the slope. It was overgrown with prickly wild roses, but here and there were openings where deer had trod narrow paths. "It's not too steep."

He shuffled the last lid to make sure it was in place. "Are you asking me to go skinny dipping?" He raised an eyebrow and took a swig of water.

Mela had to laugh. "We're too old to make a big deal about it," she teased. "Nothing special to see here."

Peter stood, holding out his hand to her. "I'll be the judge of that." Mela took his hand, and together they went to search for a path leading through the wild roses to the small beach that called to them.

CHAPTER 11

"Good luck, sweetheart." Amelie kissed Bennett's cheek and squinted at him, shading her eyes against the morning sun. "I want to know how it goes."

"It's looking good," Bennett promised. "I should seriously start looking for a place here."

"You could stay with me, of course. That's always an option." Bennett would never move in permanently, not after leading his own life for so long. It was sad, but a good thing. Few self-respecting women liked dating grown men living with their moms.

"At least in the beginning." He picked up his backpack and stepped out of the door. "In the long run, it would probably be easier for both of us if we had each other as well as our own lives."

"Yes, that would be good." Amelie smiled brightly to show she agreed. If she was lonely, it wasn't her son's responsibility to fill the void. Of course now that Mela had come back and Peter and Sunny were out and about more, it was getting difficult to feel lonely in Bay Harbor.

"Hey—what about that house you looked at?" He turned to look back. "You never mentioned it."

"It wasn't for me." Amelie felt her smile go from bright to brave and dropped it altogether.

"Uh-oh," he said. "What happened?" Bennett knew her too well to miss it.

"I have to sell this place first. Michael Wallace won't help out. And it seems to be the only house in Bay Harbor in danger of getting snapped up quickly." She shrugged.

"I guess that means it's nice?"

Amelie sighed longingly. "It's very nice. But it's okay. I already have a house."

"I think it would be good for you to move. There's a bit much..." He circled his hand at the blooming geraniums in the window boxes. "A bit much *Grandma* in this house, if you ask me."

Amelie crossed her arms. Mom had become obsessed with geraniums after taking a trip to the Alps. Amelie didn't like the lusty red or the strong smell, but she had always taken care of the plants. It was easier than facing Meredith's disappointment.

"Just that look on your face." Bennett chuckled. "You should definitely move. How about I step in? I have some savings, Mom. We can live together until this place sells, and then you can pay me back."

"Nonsense." Amelie patted his cheek. Bennett didn't make nearly as much as he should in his job. "We'll do no such thing. I'm fine; I can sort out my own finances.

Off you go, my dear. Tell the chief your mom says hi and to speed it up a bit."

"Right." Bennett went down the street where his car was parked, waving once.

Amelie waited, leaning against the door jamb and wishing geraniums wouldn't be so hardy, until Bennett drove off.

She was about to go back inside when she spotted a man getting out of his car. He'd been parked there before she and Bennett came outside. Amelie registered that he was dressed for the beach, that it was too hot to sit in a car, and that tourists didn't come to Bay Harbor.

The man came up to her gate; Amelie waited. Did he want a glass of water?

When he pushed his ball cap back and looked up, his eyes were startlingly blue in the weathered face.

She froze as the lines and planes of his features shaped a name in her mind.

He put a hand on the fence. "Hello, Amelie. Do you recognize me?"

His words thawed her knees. Amelie held on to the door. "I recognize you." Her voice sounded strange to her own ears. "What are you doing here, Charlie?"

"I guess..." He took off his cap and ran a hand through his dark hair. "I guess I was in the area and wanted to check in on Bay Harbor. I parked over there...and, well, I saw you and figured I'd say hi."

He had no idea. No idea how she'd cried over him, no idea how she'd prayed he'd get in touch, no idea how she'd cursed him. But that was years and years ago.

He was just here to check in and say hi.

"Hi," she said and exhaled a tense breath. "How are you, Charlie?"

"I'm good." He smiled. There was nothing behind that smile than politeness and small talk.

Amelie looked down.

"And you?" he asked after a pause, sounding a little puzzled. "How are you?"

"I'm fine," she replied hastily.

"Great. Well, listen, I'll be in the area for a few days, and I was wondering if you'd like to grab coffee." He shifted his weight. "I owe you an explanation and an apology."

The words felt like a shove. Almost, Amelie took a step back into the house to keep her balance. "Charles," she said, allowing herself to sound as serious as she felt. "Both explanation and apology are thirty years too late, don't you think? It hardly matters anymore."

"I'm sure it doesn't matter to you, Amelie. You moved on a long time ago. But still. The way everything happened always weighed on me. I was hoping you would let me get it off my chest." He stilled, his entire body waiting for her response.

No, thank you. At the moment, her life was complicated enough without the ghosts of her past wanting to drink coffee. Amelie opened her mouth to send him away, but then she closed it again. It didn't feel right. It would never feel right. She inhaled. "Fine. Tomorrow?"

"What about now? Do you have time?"

She smiled against her will. Overprotected and stifled, her eighteen-year-old self had loved Charlie's enthusiasm.

Amelie crossed her arms. Maybe it was better to get it over with. She'd lose sleep if she waited until tomorrow. "Okay, fine," she gave in. "Where do you want to go?"

"The Harbor Hop?" He held out his open palms in a vague gesture.

"Charlie, the Hop closed fifteen years ago. Um... There's the Beach Bistro." Amelie had had mimosas there when Mela first returned. Maybe it could be her go-to place for catching up with old friends. Old acquaintances, anyway.

"Beach Bistro? Sounds newfangled, but great. Sure." He smiled in a way that made Amelie wonder if it was wise for her to go. "My car is right over there, if I may give you a ride."

Amelie looked at the Toyota. Where had he been all these many years? From where did he come now? "Rental car?" she asked lightly.

"Yes. I flew into Bay Port," Charlie replied.

So he'd flown in. And he was only for a few days in Bay Harbor... That made everything easier. "You can use your GPS." Amelie leaned back and grabbed her purse from the coat rack beside the door. Then she came outside, closing the door behind her. "I'll take my own car and meet you there."

He nodded. "I'll see you in a few minutes, Amelie." He said it slowly as if tasting the words. Then he turned and left, walking back to his car.

He still had that easy gait that had lifted her heart so long ago.

Whatever it was, it was still there.

Chapter 12

Driving to the Beach Bistro, Amelie's head spun in circles.

Should she tell Charlie?

Would he want to know?

Would *Bennett* want him to know?

She parked, and there he was waiting, looking out at the ocean. He was dressed in board shorts and a yellow T-shirt, looking as tan as if he'd spent the last thirty years on the beach. He'd always been handsome. He could've had any girl in high school, but he picked shy, poky little Amelie, who was naive and innocent and so, so honored by his attention.

She groaned.

After all the therapy, after being a therapist herself, she still wasn't at peace with herself when it came to this man. A moment ago, she'd been in control, eager to get this over with. Now, Amelie sat in her car, alarmed over the flashbacks finding her.

Obviously, she wasn't as totally over Charlie as she'd told herself for the last twenty years. There was still more. More resentment, more anger...and more attraction.

"Stop it!" she whispered to herself. "You're a grown woman. He can't make you feel anything you don't want to feel."

Charlie had spotted her and was walking up to her car. He knocked on the roof. "Are you going to come out?"

It was only reflex that made her smile back. Her heart was drumming. Really, she wanted to leave. Get back home and curl up on the couch, watch a mind-numbing infomercial.

But if she stayed, if she talked to him—it could resolve the rest of the knot still tied around her heart. Knots were no good. And so Amelie opened the door and got out.

"Charles," she said seriously. "This isn't going to be easy. Are you sure you want to reconnect?"

He stepped back, looking embarrassed. "I've thought about you...sometimes, and I've always wondered how you were. I'd like to catch up if you're all right with it."

"Okay. Well, the bistro is over there." She slipped off her sandals.

Charlie was wearing sandals too, but they were of the flip-flop variety made for the beach. He waited for her to start walking and matched her pace.

"I almost forgot how beautiful Bay Harbor is," he said. "Look at that."

Before them stretched pure white sand, framed by soft dunes smudging into the horizon, and the shimmering sea. The glorious weather had held steady for weeks, though there were some cotton-puff clouds in the sky.

"Sit where you like," the waiter said lazily and squinted at the sun. "It's a slow day for us."

"Um, here." Amelie picked one of the bistro sets on the beach. A pretty pastel-colored market umbrella provided shade, and she wanted to bury her naked feet in the sand to ground herself.

Charlie sat as well. "What would you like?" He looked around, but the other tables were empty. "Do they serve drinks?"

"It's barely ten," Amelie said, surprised. He hadn't liked alcohol back then; it was one of the things that made him stand out from the other high school boys. But maybe she'd been naive believing him on that front too. There was a lot she had missed.

"I believe they have mimosas," she said.

"What's that again?"

"That's orange juice and champagne or prosecco," Amelie replied.

"How about...do you have champagne?" he asked the waiter who'd strolled over to their table.

"Sure do. Two glasses?"

"Yes, please."

Amelie widened her eyes in annoyance. She wanted to pay for herself, but not for champagne. She wasn't in a spending mood after the visit to the bank. "I'll just have coffee," she said coolly.

"Uh...all right." The waiter left.

Charlie didn't comment on the champagne, and Amelie wasn't sure he'd noticed.

She folded her hands on her lap and looked at the sea. "So. What brings you back to Bay Harbor? It's not exactly on the way to anything."

She heard Charlie's chair scrunch the sand as he leaned back. "Honestly? I think I came to see you, Amelie."

"Me? Why?" Her heart sped up again, and she shrugged her shoulders to make it stop. Only it didn't work.

"I never forgot you. I always wondered how you were doing."

"I'm fine."

"Of course you are." He looked at his hands. "Are you married? Any family?"

Amelie tilted her head. Far away, the dunes were golden in the afternoon light, gleaming like a dragon's hoard. But when you got there, it was only sand, shifting under your hand and running through your fingers. "Not married, no."

"No?"

"I've had my share of relationships." She straightened and looked at him.

"Oh." His face was expressionless as he looked back. No smile, no frown. Nothing.

"How about you?" she asked.

Now it was him who looked at the dunes. "Also not married. Never have been, either."

"Do you have kids?"

He shook his head. "Never made it that far."

"I have a son," Amelie said. The simple statement felt like testing the water.

"That's great. What's his name?"

She took a breath. "Bennett."

"Bennett?" He looked up. "That's a rare name. I had a grandfather who was called— "

"Yes," Amelie said. "I know."

He looked up. "Oh. Is Peter—" He blinked. "Peter isn't... Did you and he—no."

"No. Peter's one of my best friends, but we never...no."

He fell back into his chair. "Okay." He shook his head. "That's a relief."

Anger flashed through Amelie. Peter was a thousand times the better choice. "Peter is one of my best friends. And it's none of your business, anyway," she said. "You lost any right to an opinion when you left Bay Harbor without a word."

"Without a word?" Charlie tucked his chin. "But I didn't."

The waiter came and brought a bottle of champagne and flutes as well as a cup of coffee for Amelie. She nodded her thanks. Sensing something was off, the waiter quickly left again.

Amelie leaned forward. "You *didn't*?"

He opened his hands. "I wrote you a letter, Amelie."

"A letter? I didn't get a letter."

"It was... I put it in your mailbox myself."

"My mailbox? No, there was no letter, Charlie." Was he lying? He seemed genuinely confused. Amelie was confused herself. What a thing to claim.

"I sat up all night writing it, Amelie. I swear. Are you sure..." He exhaled through pursed lips. "Are you sure you didn't just forget? It's a long time ago."

Amelie put her face in her hands. "Give me a minute." There'd been a *letter*? If he really put it in her mailbox, who had taken it out?

"Amelie..." His voice changed. "Are you serious? You didn't get it?"

"I'm serious. I never got a letter."

Amelie dropped her hands. Dad had forbidden her to date Charlie. Doing it anyway had been her one act of rebellion, her guilty secret.

Would Dad have taken a letter addressed to her?

But then, what *hadn't* Dad done? His life had been a dance and his ethics his fishnet stockings. When he'd found out about prom, he'd gone to the motel to yell at Charlie's dad. But by then, Charlie had already skipped town.

"Was your name on the letter?" Amelie asked.

"Only yours," Charlie said. His voice was quiet and gray as the sea before a storm. "But I would've written it on motel stationery. It was probably easy enough to figure out who sent it to you."

"Maybe Dad did pay attention that one time." She pressed her lips in a line and shook her head.

"I had no idea. I'd have..." He ran a hand through his hair, and then he grabbed the champagne bottle and poured golden, fizzy liquid into the flutes.

"Here." He handed her one.

Amelie took it. "Cheers to your letter, Charlie," she said, not sure whether she was being sarcastic or not, and took a drink.

He did the same, grimacing as if he still didn't like alcohol. "Refreshing," he said and set his glass down.

"What did the letter say?"

"A lot, Amelie." He glanced over, his eyes full of something Amelie couldn't read. "Where to start..." He sighed. "Let's start with the reason I ran away. Remember my dad?"

"Yes, I do." Maynard Townson had been a tall man with a gaunt face who rarely talked. He'd been strict with the boys, Amelie knew.

His wife died around the time Peter graduated. Amelie had been in the audience at the graduation ceremony, and she remembered Peter missing his chance to stride across the podium and get a round of applause from his friends because the family was at the hospital to say their goodbyes.

Shortly after, Peter left for college in Portland, and things seemed to rapidly go downhill for Maynard from then on. He lost the regular guests that had kept the motel running. Charlie's jeans started to fray, and the elbows of his varsity sweaters turned threadbare even though he washed dishes at the Harbor Hop most evenings. Charlie walked over the stage to his own friends' applause, and he took Amelie to prom. But then he, too, vanished.

Years later, Maynard passed away from liver complications, and Peter returned to Bay Harbor for good. But Charlie was still gone. Not even Peter knew where he was.

"After Mom died, Dad gave up," Charlie said in a low voice. "He started drinking. It got worse and worse. Dad turned into a different person."

Compassion welled up in Amelie. "I'm sorry," she said, and the words came from her heart. "When you say he became a different person—was he bad when he drank?"

"He was." Charlie frowned. "He said I looked like Mom. Seeing me made him angry because she was gone. I think in his mind, she abandoned him. He ruined his health just so he could forget her. And there I was, taunting him with my face."

"Peter could have helped you," Amelie said quietly. Peter, too, had been angry when Amelie told him everything. But he'd also been worried.

"I was too stubborn to admit I needed help. And I was proud of him for going to college. I didn't want him to come back and lose his chance and his scholarship because I couldn't deal with Dad." Charlie refilled their glasses. "Amelie, it's all water under the bridge now. But back then, it was the reason I left. You know prom night, when we..." He looked up.

"Yes, I do." Amelie cleared her throat. "I remember." She'd had many occasions to think about that prom night. The day after turned special into stupid. The month after turned love into anger.

"Dad got me when I came home that night. He broke two of my ribs and only didn't break more because he was too drunk to aim. I wanted to be with you, Amelie. But I had to get out of Bay Harbor." He shook his head. "Maybe I would have taken it like I took the other beatings, but I'd just been with you, and it'd been so...uh. I don't know. Something more than ribs broke in me that night." He shrugged, lost for words. Amelie looked at the bubbles popping in her glass.

Eventually, Charlie continued. "I left. I hitchhiked to Bay Port, pretended I was a student at the university, and sat around the library until my ribs healed. And then I took the next flight out."

Amelie was silent, processing what he shared. He had no reason to lie, certainly not about something like that.

Unbidden, his many sports injuries came back to her. A swollen jaw, a broken finger...and he'd always been so cheerful. *No big deal. Just roughhousing with the guys... But I got 'em good, too.*

"It wasn't only the ribs, was it?" she asked.

"No." He raised his eyebrows. "I managed to keep it to myself. I played every sport I could. To get out of the house, and so I had reasons to explain my injuries. If one coach got suspicious, I could always blame another sport."

It chilled Amelie to hear. "You never thought about going to the police or a teacher?"

"I thought about it. All the time, actually," Charlie admitted. "But Dad was all right when he was sober. I always thought I could hang in, fix it somehow." He sighed. "Now I know better."

Amelie had treated children of alcoholic parents. She knew how they struggled to come to grips with tumultuous and abusive childhoods. "It takes a while to figure things out, doesn't it?" she said gently. "How are you doing now?"

"Good." He smiled a new smile. It was less flashy and more genuine. "I'm doing very well." He lifted his glass as if to drink but then sat it down again.

Amelie thought he would say something more about himself. Like what he was doing for a job, where he lived. How he lived.

Instead, he asked, "How are you, Amelie? I mean, really. How are you really?"

CHAPTER 13

"I'm also good." Amelie smiled back. "I'm struggling to grasp what you told me. I wish I had known. I wish I had gotten that letter. It would have made a difference." She tried to imagine how it would have been to know what happened to Charlie. But she couldn't.

"All this time, I thought you had read the letter. I should have known you never got it. Oh man." His sapphire eyes darkened as if clouds were crowding in. "I didn't trust you enough, Amelie."

Amelie pulled her chin back. "Why not?"

He rubbed a hand over his chin, the afternoon stubble making a rasping sound. "We were so different. You were Bay Harbor royalty. Rich, beautiful, loved. I was this beaten-down kid from the wrong side of the tracks. An abusive, alcoholic dad and a run-down motel, that's what I was. It always felt too good to be true to be dating you." He smiled wistfully. "I knew I could make you laugh, and I knew you liked me. That was my own addiction back then. I knew I had to let you go. But like Dad, I couldn't stop just because I wanted to."

"Oh." Amelie lowered her head. "I never thought of it like that. For me, there were no sides to the track. It was all just Bay Harbor, Charlie."

He pushed his glass aside. "I had nothing to offer, Amelie. Not while I was trapped in this town."

"You could have had any girl in school," Amelie remarked. "You were popular."

He waved the comment away. "All based on me faking it. I was good at sports because, believe me, I was angry. All that rage went into football and baseball and soccer."

"You were the archetypical warrior on the field but so sweet off it." Amelie pressed her lips together at the memory. She'd had no idea her boyfriend had been angry.

"I was only nice with you," he said softly. "Because you were you."

Amelie dug her feet deeper into the fine, white sand and turned to look at the shimmering water. "I had no idea, Charlie. I missed it all. I missed the entire underbelly." She shook her head. "Maybe that's why I became a therapist? Because I was missing something?"

His eyebrows flew up. "You're a therapist? Really?"

His surprise made her smile. "Yes."

"But that's perfect. I couldn't think of a better person to talk to." He laughed. "You're the most compassionate person I know."

"Not very compassionate." Amelie pushed her cold coffee aside. "I thought you left because... I thought you'd gotten what you wanted. School was over, and you were drawing a line under me."

"I was drawing a line, Amelie, but because of my Dad, not because I had gotten what I wanted. I wanted *you*."

Amelie stood. Did she trust Charlie? Did she want it all to be one huge misunderstanding, for their love back then to have been true? But if there was no letter, if he was making it up... She'd never forgive herself for letting him fool her again.

She needed to be alone for a moment. "I'll be right back."

"Of course." Charlie stood too. "Take your time."

The bathroom was cool and clean, and she washed her hands and slowly dried them, staring in the mirror.

Her mind wanted to reel, but she firmly stopped herself. If reeling was needed, there'd be time for it later. She was swimming in a sea of assumptions. She needed to get a foot on the ground, and there was only one way she could think of how to do it.

Amelie pulled out her phone and called her mother.

"Amelie," Meredith greeted her. "I've been waiting for you to call. Did you get my text? When did you last call? It feels like it's been *weeks*."

"Hi, Mom." Amelie didn't have energy to waste on little digs. She had pointed out before that Meredith could call herself if she wanted to talk. "Listen, I have a visitor. It's Charlie Townson."

"Charlie...oh, you mean Charles? That Charles? Why would you contact *him*, Amelie?"

"He contacted me."

Silence on the other end. "Well, you know best," finally came the vague response. "I've done what I could."

Meredith was unhappy with the news, of course. After explicitly forbidding Amelie to be with the boy, Meredith had held Amelie when she was sobbing tears of fear and regret.

"Mom. He said that when he left, back then... He wrote me a letter to explain why. He put it in our mailbox. Obviously, I never got it."

"A letter?" Meredith sounded confused. "What letter?"

Amelie's heart sank. "You don't know what happened to it?"

"Oh sweetheart." Suddenly, her mother's voice sounded firm. "There was no letter. I never saw one. Amelie, I know you're a grown woman now. But be careful with Charles—who knows what game he's playing this time. Don't trust him."

"I'm all right."

"Are you?"

Amelie wavered. "I think so. Would Dad have taken the letter?"

Again, there was a pause. "I don't know. He used to get the mail sometimes, and he would've checked the sender. He didn't think that boy was good for you. And for once, he was right. Look what happened."

Amelie inhaled. Breach of confidentiality aside... "Do you think he *kept* the letter? I need to know what it says.

If it is what Charlie told me—oh, Mom. It would change things."

Meredith hummed her doubt. "I don't know about that. But you sound dramatic, darling. Letter or not, he should have checked on you."

"Would Dad have kept it?" Amelie repeated.

"He was not exactly a stickler when it came to paperwork, was he? Do you want me to have a look? I still have a box or two of papers somewhere."

"Yes. Thanks, Mom. I would really, really appreciate it. Are the boxes in storage?" If they were, it would take Meredith a while to get to them.

"Well, as it happens, no. I cleaned out the storage unit."

"Oh. Good. Why?"

Meredith cleared her throat delicately. "Well, good news—I'm moving back to Bay Harbor, Amelie! Yay!"

It took a second for the meaning of the words to trickle through. Then Amelie closed her eyes and let her head sink back until it hit the tiled bathroom wall. "You're moving back? Why?"

"Because I miss you," Meredith said. "And you said Bennett is going to move back to Bay Harbor too. I thought, well, you know, time is running out. I want to see more of you two."

"Mom... You never said a word about this!"

"I sent a text, remember? I was waiting for you to call. Are you glad I'm coming?"

Amelie pulled back. "I'm glad you're coming, Mom." She meant it. It would be easier than flying to Florida to check on Meredith. "I'm glad, Mom. When are you moving?"

"End of the month, actually. It's happening quickly now."

Amelie put a hand to her forehead. "So soon. And...are you staying with me?"

"Of course," Meredith said happily. "I can't wait to see the old family home again. How are my geraniums?"

"The geraniums are fine. Mom—I'll call you back. I have to go."

"Don't wait weeks again," Meredith said. "If you do, I'll be sitting next to you on the sofa when the phone rings."

"Yes. No. I'll call tonight. Bye, Mom."

"Lots of love, darling. Can't wait to live in the same house again."

Amelie wondered if it was true or a veiled threat. "Love you too," she replied weakly. "Bye."

She ended the call. What was happening? Had she accidentally manifested a total upheaval of her life? She stepped out of the bathroom, and there was Charlie, taking his credit card back from the waiter.

When he spotted her, relief softened his jaw. "Amelie, are you all right?"

She had no idea whether she was all right. "I had to call Mom."

"I thought you left," he admitted with a small laugh that tugged on Amelie's heart.

"I'm here," she said and spontaneously hooked her arm under his. "I do have to get back home, though. But

I'm free this evening. Do you want to go somewhere for dinner?" She smiled up at him. She remembered those eyes and lips. She remembered everything about his face even though it had changed. And she remembered how much she'd loved this man.

It was easy to forget, but in the end, everyone had to choose who they wanted to be. Angry, resentful...or loving and kind. Whatever had happened, whether he was a liar or truthful, he was Charlie.

"I would love that." He put a hand on hers. "Thank you, Amelie."

"I want to know more about you," she said as they went to the exit. "And I have something to tell you, too."

Chapter 14

Kimmie touched the sandy bottom and pushed off, propelling herself back toward the rippling, shimmering surface. The blue around her became brighter and lighter until finally, she broke through the water. She shook her wet hair back and then swam toward the beach until the water was too shallow. She waded the rest, waving to Sisley.

Her sister, dressed in a floaty maxi dress, was taking a short beach break from nursing and changing nappies.

"Hey." Kimmie fell on her towel beside Sisley's, turned on her belly, and rested her head on her arm. A relaxed, happy feeling came over her.

"Hey," Sisley said, propping herself up on her elbow. "How was it?"

"Fabulous." Kimmie yawned. "But now I could fall asleep."

"Me too." Sisley chuckled.

"I bet. You were awake all night. I can hear you creaking around on the wood floor. I thought we had a ghost."

"Do I keep you up?" In true sisterly fashion, Sisley sounded amused, not sorry.

Kimmie rolled on her back, letting the midmorning sun dry the saltwater on her skin. "I keep myself up," she said and lazily fished for her sunglasses in the beach bag. Sisley was wearing hers, together with a wide straw hat to protect her skin. Kimmie had a tan and rarely got sunburned anymore.

"Why?"

"Just...work stuff."

"I read your last article," Sisley said. "I don't know how you can stand going to these places. It's awful."

"It is," Kimmie replied. The last project had been the toughest yet. It lasted months, and the stress of reporting on the human cost of war had robbed her of more than her sleep. "But someone has to report what's happening."

"I wish it didn't have to be you though."

Kimmie shaded her face with a hand. "I do too—multiple times a day."

"Do something else then."

"The people need a voice. Their reality deserves to be witnessed just as much as a celebrity's. More. And someone has to do it."

"You're like Bennett," Sisley said. "He said the same thing about someone having to do the job."

"Did you talk to him?" Kimmie looked up.

"He called yesterday," Sisley said. "He wanted to know how the baby is. I think he really cares."

Kimmie nodded.

So Bennett was calling her sister. He'd never called her. Sadness spread, cold and flat, in her chest, cloaking the relaxed happiness she'd felt. Kimmie sat up and pulled on a T-shirt, then hugged her knees. The water had dried, leaving salt on her skin.

"I'm sorry," Sisley said quietly. "He just asked how I was and how the baby was doing. That was it. I'm not interested in getting between you two or anything."

Kimmie tried to smile. "I saw how he looked at you, Sis," she replied. "I don't think it's you who is getting between anything."

"What do you mean?" Sisley raised her eyebrows, alarmed. "Girl, I'm not looking. Believe me."

"It's all right." Kimmie sighed dramatically. "You two would make a great pair."

There was a long pause. "I thought you liked him," Sisley said finally. "Aside from the fact that I'm going to stay single, I thought you liked him."

Kimmie pushed her sunglasses up. "I do. I would like to date him, to be honest."

"So why don't you?" Sisley looked surprised as if all Kimmie had to do was snap her fingers and men would ask her out.

"Because I don't think he's at all interested," Kimmie said reasonably. "Sad as that is."

"Of course he's interested," Sisley said loyally. "You're a famous journalist with serious skills, and you look like a short-haired Lara Croft. Any man would want to date you." She smiled.

"Your confidence is touching," Kimmie said. "And thank you for the Lara Croft comparison. But...believe it or not, it's not happening."

"Maybe they're intimidated."

"Maybe. Or maybe it's just me they don't like." Kimmie looked at her sister. "Sis, I couldn't even keep my husband."

A gull screamed and plunged toward the water. In the shade of her hat, Sisley frowned. "So? I shouldn't have stayed with Lars. Seems pretty obvious now, but honestly, we have a lot less control over our lives than we think."

"I guess."

"So maybe *you* kept Travis and he lost *himself*," Sisley offered. "Maybe the divorce is *his* fault."

"Hmm."

Sisley leaned closer. "Whose fault was it? You never said. I only have that one text saying he left, and you were getting a divorce."

"I never said because I don't know." Kimmie sighed. "I'd like to tell you all the dirty secrets, Sis. It'd be easier if there were some. But the truth is I don't know why he left."

Sisley's mouth opened.

"I *know*," Kimmie said, smiling at the reaction. Kimmie would keep quiet if it'd been anyone else but Sis with her own failed relationship. But her sister understood. Kimmie took a breath. "I came home from a trip one day, and he was gone. He left divorce papers on the nightstand."

"He did? Whoa. That's rough."

"I should've called him, Sis." Kimmie looked up at her younger sister. "I was in shock. I was angry. I'd just come back from a war zone and couldn't keep it together any longer. So instead of calling him, I signed his stupid papers and sent them to my lawyer. Just like that, as if our marriage meant nothing at all."

Sisley's face softened with compassion. Kimmie lowered her head. "I'm kind of ashamed I did that," she murmured. "I don't know why I always act so tough. I really loved him."

"I know one reason why you act tough," Sisley said, but she said it kindly.

Kimmie looked up. She'd been hard on Sisley, too. She remembered her sister's whining and the timid ways that were so different from her own but had forgotten about Sisley's kindness, compassion, and loyalty. She tried to smile. "Yeah? Why do I act tough? Let's hear it."

"For one, look at what you do for a living," Sisley answered. "It's hard to even read the things you witness. You can't step into a crisis situation and soak up everyone's despair. It would crush you. You have to be tough to be their messenger. It's your *job* to protect your heart with top-notch armor. I'm talking plate armor. Iron. Shields and spikes everywhere. The works."

Kimmie nodded; there was something to what Sisley said. Nowadays, divorce papers were hardly a tragedy. It was easy to downplay what happened in her own comfortable life after witnessing true suffering. "Maybe I protected myself so well, Travis was left standing alone."

"Maybe. Maybe he should have helped you dismantle your armor. Who knows?"

Kimmie pressed her lips together. "Then again, I've always been like this. Even as a kid. Even to you and Morris. Maybe something's wrong with me."

Sisley took off her sunglasses and shook her head, exasperated. "I'm sorry, what? Do you even remember how it was at home?"

Startled, Kimmie looked up. "How was what at home? We had a great childhood."

"Well, Mom was trying her best. But how do you feel when you think of Travis?"

"Sad?" Kimmie said, slightly taken aback at her sister's outburst. They did have a great childhood. They'd had everything they wanted. Vacation in Aruba, all the gadgets and toys, Mom reasonably available.

"How else do you feel?"

"Oh man. Um. Abandoned, betrayed... He should've given me a chance to talk face to face. Maybe a warning. Something."

"So you feel abandoned. When you were a child, who else made you feel like that?" Sisley's energy had simmered down. She was watching Kimmie as if she genuinely wanted to know.

"Well..." It didn't take long to recognize the feeling. "Dad, I suppose. I was always hoping he'd be there, you know."

"But mostly, he wasn't."

"To be fair, he tried," Kimmie said quickly.

"I'm not blaming him," Sisley said. "But this is not about him. It's about you—and maybe even me and Morris. I was so used to begging for scraps of love that I stuck with *Lars*." She cleared her throat and put her sunglasses back on. "You want something to be ashamed of?" Sisley said, voice wavering. "Try letting someone manipulate you into keeping your pregnancy a secret."

"I'm sorry, Sisley," Kimmie said. She wanted to make it better, to get back the beautiful summer day they'd enjoyed only a minute ago.

"It's okay." Sisley rubbed her cheek. "All lessons to be learned."

Kimmie reached out and touched her sister's shoulder. "And when did you become so wise?"

"I'm not wise." Sisley lay back down, putting her hat over her eyes. "I'm one hundred percent making it up as I go along. But you do look like Lara Croft."

"Well, that's the most important thing." Kimmie sat quietly for a while, thinking about Travis, and Lars. "Hey, Sis?" she said eventually.

"What?" Sis asked.

"Since you are on a roll—how do we avoid more of the same thing? I don't want to have a pattern. If we can't control what the men in our lives do, which, apparently, we can't... Should we stop dating altogether?"

"Dibs on that strategy," Sisley replied. "But if that doesn't work for you, date, talk, and don't abandon yourself the way I did. Give yourself what you need. Imagine talking to your eight-year-old self. And then, as a grown, capable woman, give her what she needs. Love, attention..."

"That trip to the waterpark Dad never made time for..." Kimmie grinned.

Sisley nodded. "If you take care of her, nobody else needs to fill that hole in your heart. Nobody else can, anyway."

Kimmie lay back down. "The waterpark I can do, but the rest is easier said than done," she murmured. "How do you show up for yourself?"

Sisley's reply came on a sleepy exhale. "You nap on the beach."

Kimmie blinked; her eyelids were heavy too. "We're on a straight road to healing then." The nights of lost sleep were catching up with Kimmie. She felt back in control.

Bennett wasn't meant for her. Her attraction to the man had been just a desperate grab for attention, a Band-Aid to cover up what she really needed.

"I know," Sisley whispered, and it was the last thing Kimmie heard before she fell asleep.

In her dream, she picked up the phone and called Travis. And in her dream, Travis had been waiting for the call.

CHAPTER 15

Sunny set the bottle of aloe vera on the kitchen counter. "Try this," she said with all the exasperation of someone who *told* you so.

Kimmie glanced guiltily at Sisley. They had both dozed off. She was fine, but her sister's skin was starfish-red where the hat hadn't protected her. At least Mom and a very hungry Lovie found them before Sisley burned to a crisp.

Sisley shifted Lovie to her other hip and picked up the bottle. "Thanks, Sunny. I'll put it on right now." She left, humming to the baby.

"I'm making you something proper to eat," Sunny declared. "You're both of you run down to fall asleep on the beach like that."

"Eating always helps," Kimmie teased. "Even when you're sleep-deprived, not hungry."

More than her long nap, the talk with Sisley had made her feel better. They were both in a new place. Things would be better now they'd connected.

"You're hungry all right; you barely touched breakfast before running off. What do you feel like, Kimmie?" Sunny hobbled busily to the fridge.

"Anything is great. But I'll make lunch. You sit down for a change."

Sunny waved her off. "I've been sitting all morning. I want to move."

"You just don't want anyone else to mess up your kitchen." Despite her hip, Sunny had taken charge of most of the cooking and baking.

Sunny pulled packages from the fridge and set them by the stoves. "Can you blame me? I've sat in a motel room for two years, dreaming of cooking a decent meal. I have a lot of catching up to do."

"Peter would have let you cook in the motel." Kimmie handed her great-aunt the big pan from the cabinet.

"Ah, I can't climb stairs, child. And I was too heavy. It made it even harder."

"You've lost more weight," Kimmie observed. Sunny's preferred house attire, a burgundy, velvet sweat suit Mom had found in a local boutique, used to stretch across the belly. Now, it hung in folds.

"The doctor will be happy." Sunny lit the stove. "I have an appointment this afternoon. I want this surgery off my list."

"I know," Kimmie said and opened the packages from the meat counter. There were thick slices of ham inside. "You'll have to be a little patient afterward and do what the doctor says."

"If I need your advice, I'll ask." Sunny slapped the ham into the pan.

"It'll be all right," Kimmie said mildly. Sunny was afraid of the anesthetic. She didn't admit it, but everyone knew anyway. "They do so many of these surgeries, they know what they're doing. You'll see."

"Do you want an egg with your ham?"

"Yes, please. Sis will have one too, please."

Sunny set to work. She had recently fallen in love with the yummy food depictions in Japanese children's anime and decided to copy the meals in real life. Steaming bowls of luscious ramen noodles topped with ham and eggs sunny-side up, rice rolls with sweet bean filling, sushi, mochi cakes, delicate miso soups—if it was pretty and full of flavor, it was quickly becoming part of the household's lunch routine.

Kimmie loved everything about the situation, from Sunny's adoring children's anime to eating the food. "I should get the key to my house today," she said, fetching the new set of soup bowls. "I hope it works out. My real estate agent was going to call and confirm."

"Ooh. Exciting!" Sunny scooped curly ramen noodles into the bowls. She'd found them online and ordered one for Sis and Kimmie each. They were painted with yawning cats and had holes to hold chopsticks. After the noodles had been arranged, Sunny ladled her homemade broth, slipped a slice of roasted ham and egg on top, and sprinkled toasted sesame seeds over it all.

Kimmie sat and picked up her spoon. The warm scent curling into the air made her stomach rumble. "You're right, I'm starving," she said, surprised. "It smells fabulous, and it looks great, too. Thank you, Sunny."

"You're very welcome, child. Sisley!" Sunny called out. "Lunch is ready!"

"Where is Mom?" Kim tasted the steaming soup. "The broth is so good. What did you put in it?"

"I started with a basic Pho soup recipe," Sunny said. "But I made it my own. Good?"

Kimmie swapped the spoon for chopsticks and expertly broke off a piece of ham, dipping it into the egg. "Very good. Please write that recipe down." She looked up. "What happened to Mom? Is she not eating with us?"

"She wanted to check the bees," Sunny said and tried a noodle. "A couple of colonies lost their queens."

"What is she going to do about that?"

"She got a couple of new queens in the mail this morning. They have to be put into the colonies. Hopefully, the bees will accept them."

"Why wouldn't they?" Kimmie wrapped long strands of ramen with her chopstick.

Sunny took the empty pot to the sink. "They're not about to work for just any old queen; it has to be their mom."

"Goodness. Kind of hard to fake, is it?"

"Mela put the new queens in cages sealed with sugar plugs. By the time the bees chew their way through, the queens should smell like the colonies."

Sisley appeared in the door, glistening with aloe vera gel. Sunny waved her over. "I can take Lovie," she said, and Sisley handed her the baby.

"Why don't you sit down with her?" Sisley asked. "We'll clean up after we're done." She led Sunny to her recliner and then joined Kimmie in the kitchen to eat.

Kimmie had barely eaten the last piece of ham when her phone buzzed. She snapped it up. "Ian's calling about the house!" Eagerly, she answered. "Yes?"

"It's on," Ian said. "I have the keys. Can you meet me at the house in an hour?"

"Oh my goodness!" Kimmie pumped a fist into the air. "I'll be there! I can't wait!"

Ian laughed. "Congratulations, homeowner!"

"Thank you! See you at one o'clock." Kimmie jumped up. "Sunny, I'm going to get cleaning supplies. Do you need anything from the market?"

"Fresh shrimp for dinner if they have."

Kimmie made a quick market run to get a broom, mop, soaps, and dust cloths. She also tossed towels into the mix, bed linens, a pillow and blanket, even two sets of dishes and glasses from the seasonal aisle. Her excitement grew with every minute that ticked by. Her own house!

She remembered Sunny's shrimp and was back at 12 Seasweet Lane in half an hour, stowing the shrimp in the fridge. Then she drove to 5 Seasweet Lane and parked. Ian hadn't arrived yet.

Her phone buzzed before she could get out.

Had something gone wrong after all? Was this a last-minute cancellation?

Kimmie checked the screen, but the caller had already hung up. She didn't recognize the number, and a quick reverse-lookup showed it to be private.

It could literally be anybody. A butt dial, a glitch of the thumb... She sighed. Why did her thoughts immediately jump to Travis?

He of all people wouldn't call. Not out of the blue like this. Or at all.

Would he?

Kimmie tapped into her contacts and hovered over his old number, just to see how it felt. Then she pressed. Her hand trembled when she held the phone to her ear.

"I'm sorry," a woman's voice informed her. "Your call cannot be completed as dialed."

Kimmie let her phone sink. Travis had changed his phone number after the divorce. Unlike her, he'd moved on.

She looked again at the unknown number. Who had called her?

CHAPTER 16

Lovie was warm and limp by the time Sisley had fed and changed her. Sisley softly lowered the baby onto the crib mattress, hoping she wouldn't jostle awake, closed the curtain against the bright sun, and sat with a book on the glider. On her side table stood a mason jar full of iced lemon water and a vase overflowing with pink fairy roses. She picked up the jar and sipped from the pretty paper straw.

How lucky she was to be here... She had jumped out of the frying pan, but instead of freefalling into the fire, her mother had snatched her to safety.

Lovie made a snuffling sound. She only wore a onesie, and her sprawling arms and legs were the cutest things.

Sisley leaned back gingerly, adjusting the straps of her loose dress. Her sunburn brought back the talk with her sister. They'd never really connected before, but Kimmie was much more approachable here in Bay Harbor.

Far from being a relationship expert, Sisley feared that Kimmie was right about Bennett. The way he sometimes looked at Sisley suggested he wasn't interested in more than a friendship with Kimmie.

Well, Sisley wasn't interested in glances. Bennett was nice and certainly helpful and also generous and kind...but she was going to stay single. After Lars, it was hard to want another relationship. It was best to stand on her own two feet.

She rocked back and forth for a while, watching Lovie sleep.

Her next step was to find a job and get out of the house. Mom needed space to focus on herself. Kimmie and Morris were adults who earned their own money and lived grown-up lives, and Sisley was going to do the same.

Sisley stopped rocking. She picked up the baby monitor and quietly went into her own room. Unlike the dim nursery, it was flooded with sunlight, and a bird was singing sweetly by the open window. Sisley glanced out at the apple trees. Gnarly and knobby with age, they were a haven for birds and critters, and there, on the highest branch of the closest tree, sat a goldfinch. Peter said they were just starting to nest.

Sisley watched it for a while, then she went to open her laptop, pulled up her college site, and logged into her old student account.

She hadn't finished her arts degree. Classes became more and more difficult to sit through; homework had felt like a straitjacket. Graphic design, photography, art history... The thing she'd loved to do was painting. But her professor hated everything she put on paper.

She tried to do better, liking her paintings less and less. In the end, her professor announced to the entire class that his four-year-old could produce a better landscape than her. Sisley had bitten her lip so hard she'd tasted blood. Then she'd collected her things and left the classroom, only breathing again when she stepped outside.

Well, maybe she'd been right to stop. It was tough to make money as an artist. Even for a talented painter it was a hard, long slog to build an audience large enough to make a living. There were no guarantees, and Sisley knew she was more of a quitter than a fighter.

But it was different now.

Lovie deserved a stable home. It was Sisley's job to make sure she had it.

Sisley stood and reached for the watercolors on the shelf. She opened them and ran a fingertip over the dry pigment cakes. The sunlight made the colors come alive.

She pulled out the European brushes with the fine badger hairs, tracing patterns on the inside of her wrist. They were a gift from Mom and Dad. She'd rarely used them, preferring cheaper hog-hair brushes because she wasn't that good. Not good enough for good brushes.

She frowned, pressing down harder, drawing tighter circles on the sensitive skin.

The professor had no right to tell her off. How was she to learn? Not everyone came out of the gate a perfect artist. The point was to learn.

Lars had been the same. She was never good enough for him.

"Screw that," she whispered and lifted the brush before the fine hairs would bend. "From now on, I will do what *I* want."

So she wasn't going to make a living. She could get a job at the local market; they were looking for someone to work the register. It would earn enough to provide food and shelter for Lovie. Dad had promised to help with college, just like he would help Kimmie's and Morris's kids if they had any. It was enough. It was more than enough.

She was enough.

She laid the brush on the table as a reminder.

As soon as she was healed from giving birth, she would get a job in Bay Harbor to pay the bills. And she was going to paint whatever she wanted, however she wanted, using her best brushes.

Sisley opened a sketchbook and picked up a pencil. Then she went back to the window.

The goldfinch was gone from the tree, but Sisley could picture him perfectly. She started sketching, letting herself sink into the strokes and hatches and stipples to create form and softness and light and something more, something she felt, not saw.

Tears dropped from Sisley's wide-open eyes onto the paper, blurring lines and changing contours as if the universe had decided to take part in shaping her creation. She blinked them away, impatient to complete the sketch.

"Sisley? What's going on?"

Sisley startled. "Mom."

"Hey." Mom's shirt sleeves were folded to the elbows, her navy capri pants were streaked with wax and honey, and she smelled of bees and smoke and apples. "Are you okay?"

"I'm...drawing," Sisley said. The words felt wooden on her tongue. The sketchbook in her arm sank as her muscles relaxed. "I was drawing, Mom," she said, surprised at how good she felt. She hadn't noticed her mood change. "It was wonderful."

"Oh, great." Mom smiled tersely. "You always were so talented. I wish you had better luck with your professors."

Sisley turned the pencil in her fingers. "I don't know, Mom. Maybe he was right. Anyway. I've decided to get a job in Bay Harbor and just paint for myself."

"Paint for me too, please." Mom came into the room and hugged Sisley. "It's time to take down my childhood drawings downstairs and put up your pretty ones instead."

Sisley laughed. "I say wait until Lovie can help us out."

"You look happy." Mom let her go.

"I am happy, Mom. I feel like you saved me."

"Oh baby. Anytime."

Sisley took a breath. "Mom, would you like to see the drawing?"

Her mother's throat moved. "Can I?"

Sisley nodded. She'd not shown any of her work to anyone in two or maybe even three years. She'd felt too embarrassed about it. But she'd share with Mom.

Sisley pinched her eyes shut. It felt as if she were six years old again, vulnerable and out of control. "Um. Tell me the truth, Mom, yeah? If you don't like it, it's okay. I'll keep doing it, but I want to do it just for myself then."

"Okay."

"Honest truth, even if it's silly."

"Honest truth, darling. It's not silly. I will tell you exactly what I think. You deserve to make your own decision about sharing your art."

Sisley held out her sketch.

"Sisley," Mom said quietly. Sisley felt the book tugged from her hands. "Sis, this is *beautiful*. This is... What *is* it?"

Sisley opened an eye. "It's a bird on a tree, Mom. Are you being serious?"

Her mother laughed. "If it is, it's abstract, Sisley. I mean, have a look yourself."

And for the first time, Sisley looked.

There wasn't the simple, heartfelt image of a finch on a tree she'd thought she was putting on the paper. There were forms and shapes and...love?

"Oh. Huh," Sisley said, surprised. She'd never before drawn a feeling.

When she looked up, Mom's eyes were shining. "Can I have this, Sis? I want to frame it."

"You don't—" Sisley stopped herself. She'd meant to say, *have to do that.*

But that was little Sisley talking, the child holding up a picture to Dad, who, without looking at it, told her to tell Mom to frame it and please knock on the door next time she came into the office.

The advice she'd shared with her sister on the beach came back to Sisley.

Nobody but you can fill the hole in your heart.

She looked again at the sketch. What Mom saw in it, she didn't know. But to her, the lines looked as if a river had poured from her fingers onto the paper, the waves carrying pieces of her soul like a flood carrying tree branches. Good or bad or crazy or weird... It was *enough*.

"I mean it, Sis." Mom frowned. "I'm not being polite. I love it."

"I believe you." Sisley felt a smile spread on her lips. "I like it too. It's yours if you want it."

"Looking at this makes me... I don't know. Happy."

Before, the words would have bounced off the walls Sisley had built long ago to protect herself. Now, she heard them. "Thank you, Mom," Sisley said quietly. "For everything."

"Come downstairs with me." Mom put an arm around Sisley. "Let's all have lemonade on the patio. I want to show Sunny the drawing."

CHAPTER 17

Sisley was in the kitchen, pouring the icy lemonade into glasses, when the doorbell rang. She looked up, wiping a drop from the spout.

"I'll get it," Mom called from the patio.

Sisley carried the drinks outside and set them on the table. The sun was still high in the sky, and the sky was spotlessly blue. She opened the large market umbrella over the table.

"What a beautiful drawing this is, sweetheart," Sunny said, studying the bird in the tree that was no bird in a tree. At least not to the casual observer. "I love everything about it."

Sisley leaned over her great-aunt's shoulder. "It's upside down!" She laughed. "See? This is a tree." She turned the drawing and traced the shape with a finger.

"Oh." Sunny chuckled. "Now I see it. But honestly, I don't care which way around I look at it. Keep making these, please."

"I will. I'm still worried about what people think of them," Sisley confessed. "But I won't let it stop me anymore."

"Ah, people." Sunny waved a hand as if humanity were a fly. "Do what you like with your one beautiful life. You can never make all of them happy. If you can make yourself happy, you're well ahead of the curve."

"And Lovie." Sisley sat down. "I plan on making her happy, too. I'm going to get a job at the market. Or maybe the Beach Bistro needs another waitress."

Sunny threw her a searching look. "How about asking your dad for help? He's swimming in money. He can share."

Sisley shook her head. "He's already going to pay for Lovie's college, and he's paid for mine. It's more than most get. I should handle the rest."

"And you'll be fine. Just make sure to get a job that lets you do *this*." Sunny put the drawing on the table and weighed it down with the book she'd been reading.

"Hi, you two." Amelie came out on the balcony, carrying one of the enormous cake stands she seemed to own in limitless supply. Leaning between them, Amelie pressed a kiss first on Sisley's, then on Sunny's cheek. "What a beautiful day, isn't it?"

"Well, you're in a good mood," Sunny said.

"I brought cake," Amelie announced the obvious and set it on the table.

"How am I supposed to lose weight when you keep bringing goodies? What is it?" Sunny lifted the opaque dome.

"Blueberry cheesecake, freshly baked by yours truly. It's a German recipe, and I made it just for you."

"How is German cheesecake different from American?" Sisley asked, inhaling the cake's sweet scent. She and Kimmie lucked out with Sunny and Amelie being in a constant bake-off.

"It's fluffier and lighter, and it's de-li-cious."

"Hello again," came a deep voice from the patio door. "How is everyone?"

Sisley looked up. Her eyes met Bennett's.

"Bennett, I'm trying to lose weight," Sunny said bossily. "Tell your mother to stop baking these cakes. If they're on the table, I must eat them. I have to go to the doc later and step on that scale."

"Stop baking, Mother," Bennett said pleasantly and smiled at Sisley.

"Hi, Bennett," she said. "It's nice to see you again." Her face warmed, and she averted her eyes. She was still embarrassed that she'd spoiled his car seat, even though Mom had insisted on having it professionally cleaned in Sandville. Lars would've been so mad. Bennett wasn't like that. But her body needed time to heal from more than giving birth.

"It's nice to see you too," he replied. "How are you recovering?"

"Fine. It's fine. I'm fine." Sisley rose, unsuccessfully willing the heat in her cheeks away. "Would you like lemonade?"

She went inside without waiting for an answer, holding her breath until she was safely in the kitchen. "No no *no*," she whispered to herself as she took the pitcher from the fridge. "No!"

"Are you all right?"

Sisley wheeled around. Mom was standing at the door, eyebrows raised in concern.

"It's Bennett," Sisley whispered and poured. "I think I like him. And I don't want to." Her hand wobbled, and she spilled lemonade on the counter.

Mom went to get a dishcloth and wiped it up. "He's very nice," she whispered back. "He brought you to the hospital. Don't be silly." Then her eyes widened. "Oh." The hand holding the cloth pointed at Sisley. "Like, like-like?"

"But I don't want to. I'm glad I got rid of Lars, I have a brand-new baby, I'm not looking. At all."

"I think you're right. You'll need time, sweetheart." Mom smiled fondly and washed out the cloth in the sink. "Best to let Bennett know one way or the other."

Sisley threw a glance over her shoulder, just in case more people came in. "Just so we're on the same page, Mom... It's not like he's said anything, right? I'm talking strictly about myself."

"Aha. Well, then, best to give yourself a little talking-to."

"That's exactly what I was doing."

"I see." Mom hung the dishcloth over the side of the sink with an amused flourish of her wrist. Then she got out cake plates and forks and went back outside. Sisley followed with the glasses.

Amelie and Bennett were seated on either side of Sunny. Bennett looked up only briefly when she came out, helping to dole out plates and napkins and forks.

Sisley set her load down and went to her chair. She was wearing one of Grandma Julie's loose hippie dresses. Was her baby belly still showing? She stopped herself. It didn't matter, did it? Nobody was interested in the way she looked. She picked up the monitor instead, shading the small screen so she could see Lovie.

"Is that a video monitor?" Bennett pulled out the chair across the table from her and sat.

Sisley looked up. "Yes, it is," she said and turned the monitor to show the screen.

"May I see?"

"Sure." She handed him the gadget. Amelie leaned over as well, and they put their heads together.

"Oh my goodness, she's the most precious baby I've ever seen in my *life*," Amelie said, and it sounded so heartfelt both Bennett and Sisley burst out laughing.

As if on cue, the baby stirred.

Sisley tilted her head. "Would you like to go get her?" she offered.

"Lifting a sleepy baby from the crib is a treat," Mom promised.

Sisley saw Amelie inhale to accept, but Bennett was first. "I'd love to," he said, handed his mother the monitor, stood, and disappeared inside.

There was a moment of stunned silence, then Amelie said, "Mela?"

It was Mom's turn to burst out laughing. "How about that? Your son loves babies. Just what you always wanted."

"He likes Lovie because he basically delivered her," Sunny said.

"He didn't basically deliver her," Sisley protested. "He only drove me to the hospital."

"I don't know," Amelie said fondly. "He was a nervous wreck when I got there. He might be more invested than you realize."

No, was all Sisley could think. No, *no*, no. No.

Mom looked at her, barely suppressing more laughter, but she was also shaking her head.

"Listen." Amelie put the baby monitor on the table. "Is he humming?"

"He is." Sunny laughed. "Sis, you should make him godfather. He's a keeper."

"Oh Sisley, do make him godfather. He would love it. I've never seen him like this," Amelie chimed in, eyes shining. "I promise he's great with kids. He'll always be there for Lovie."

"I'll think about it," Sisley said weakly.

Bennett came back out, Lovie in his arms and a besotted look on his face. Sisley was glad Amelie was telling them about her mother Meredith leaving Florida and moving back to Bay Harbor.

Okay. It didn't help enough.

Nobody noticed when Sisley stood to meet Bennet. Nobody saw the look he gave her as she came to him or felt the beat of her heart. And nobody knew that when Bennett handed her the baby, Sisley felt he and Lovie were the two most perfect human beings she had ever met.

Of course, it was all just hormones going haywire. An oxytocin overdose. No wonder they called it the love hormone. It would stop messing with her head and heart any day now. She just had to get to the other side to be free from random crushes.

Lovie smelled as sweet and clean as the first page in a brand-new sketchbook, but Sisley hurried inside to change her diaper anyway.

CHAPTER 18

After Amelie and Bennet left, Mela changed from her beekeeping clothes into a summer dress and drove to the motel. Peter had texted earlier, saying he was going to start gutting the rooms on the upper level. Mela hadn't seen him since the day before and already missed him. She only had a few minutes before taking Sunny to her appointment in Bay Port, but it was enough to say hi.

The motel courtyard was blocked by a container for renovation debris. Mela parked on the street and went inside, where she found Peter brooding in front of the computer. He rubbed his hands over his face and then rounded the counter to pull her into a bear hug.

Mela put a hand on his arm. "I saw Amelie after lunch, and she told me something interesting. I don't know if you heard yet, Peter, but I have permission to share."

"Heard what?" He looked at her sternly. "Has Robert come for you? I'll fight him."

"Robert's got a new girlfriend he likes very much. She's half my age and three times as pretty."

"That's crazy talk, woman."

"She's smart too. Even I like her." Mela smiled. "Do you want to sit in the yard?"

"I want you to tell me right now what Amelie said, but okay. Can I get you a beer?"

"It's barely three o'clock. You go ahead and have one. I'm sure you've earned it."

"I don't know about that, but I'll have one anyway."

He went to the fridge in the breakfast room and pulled out a green bottle, and then they went to the backyard together, where there was a bench surrounded by night-blooming jasmine and bougainvilleas in large terracotta pots, honeysuckle, and wisteria vines. An old boxwood hedge hid the sea, but Mela heard the rushing of the waves.

They sat side by side, and Peter put his bottle on the ground. "So, what news did you want to tell me?"

"Amelie was over at my house earlier today. She had a visitor early this morning." Mela knew Peter avoided talking about Charlie, but not why. Something had happened between the two brothers.

"And who was the visitor?" Peter raised an eyebrow at her dillydallying.

"It was your brother, Charlie," Mela said carefully.

Peter slowly turned his head as if he hadn't heard right. "*Charlie?*"

"Yes. That's what Amelie said."

"He's...unexpected," Peter murmured after a while.

"I'm not sure what's going on with you and Charlie," Mela said softly. "Are you glad he's back?"

"Uh." Peter shook his head. "How was Amelie?"

"She seemed in a good mood, happy and bubbly and hands full of cheesecake." Mela thought back to her friend's visit. "I thought it was because Bennett is in Bay Harbor."

Peter sat silently, staring at nothing.

"What happened between you and Charlie?"

Peter put an arm around her and pulled her closer. "It's not so much about Charlie and *me*."

Mela straightened so she could look at him. "Charlie and *Amelie*?"

Peter nodded.

"And you can't tell because..." She frowned.

Peter raised an eyebrow as if it was obvious.

Amelie and Charlie... Something that happened between them, something big enough for Amelie to swear Peter to secrecy—Mela sank back. "Are you serious?"

Peter narrowed his eyes as if trying to guess what was going on in her brain. "Probably."

Mela put a hand on her head. "Why didn't she tell me?"

"I'm fairly sure she didn't see a reason why. I promised to keep her secret. You're the first one to make me break my promise." He kissed her head. "I've always wanted to tell you."

"You haven't told me anything—only dropped hints. But that's enough. It explains why nobody ever talks about Charlie."

"Yup."

"So—what exactly happened?"

With a sigh, Peter reached for his bottle, twisted off the top, and took a drink. "Charlie took Amelie to prom—and he allowed things to go further than he should've. Unlike him, Amelie was seriously in love. She thought he was the one. Next thing she knew, Charlie skipped town."

"Poor Amelie." Mela knew her friend had grown up protected, but she wasn't the first girl to mistake prom music for wedding bells.

"I was in college in Bay Port. Amelie reached out to me when she found out she was...you know. She was hoping Charlie was couch-crashing at my place. But he wasn't." Peter frowned. "She had to tell her parents... Believe me when I say Charlie left a huge mess. I was almost as angry at him as Amelie's dad. I tried to help her as best I could, but I was a broke student without a car and there wasn't much I could do. I worked extra hours just to pay the phone bill. For a while we talked a lot."

"I'm sure that helped her a little." Mela leaned her head on his shoulder. "Did you ever hear from Charlie again? I get that you were angry, but were you worried?"

For a moment, Peter looked nauseated. He exhaled slowly. "I was more than worried. After I graduated, I came back here to stay with Dad."

Mela could still remember the tall man with the large, bony hands. She'd been wary of him. When she was old enough to wonder why, she figured it was because he was different from the only other men in her life. Her uncle Finn, who was funny and flew kites on the beach, and her teacher Mr. Gordon, who wore glasses and wrote songs they had to sing.

"How did your dad feel about Charlie?" she asked.

"That's the thing. He was hopping mad. But Charlie was only eighteen, and he had disappeared." He held her gaze. "Dad wasn't worried about him. Not one bit. It scared me."

"Maybe he knew something more? Did he know where Charlie was and keep it to himself?"

"Not as angry as he was." Peter shook his head. "Even before, the two were butting heads."

"Was it difficult for you?"

"I pretended I had a handle on things, but I didn't. Amelie's parents wouldn't let me anywhere near her. Dad was...slipping. I wanted to look for Charlie, but Dad refused to help. We got in some pretty bad fights." He sighed. "I couldn't deal with his addiction and his anger, and then he told me to get out. So I did. I got out all the way to Africa."

"I'm sorry." Did Peter wonder all these years whether his dad had something to do with Charlie's disappearance?

Peter put the bottle back on the ground. "I don't want my beer anymore, thinking back on Dad." He picked a sprig of jasmine and stared at it with unseeing eyes. "Now you know how the business got run into the ground."

"Well, Charlie's back, and he's fine," Mela murmured. "Amelie said he looked good."

Peter didn't respond.

"The first thing he did was find Amelie to apologize. They talked this morning."

"How did she take it?" He looked up.

"She seemed happy when I saw her. Bennett was the same as always."

"That's good. Did she say anything else?"

"We couldn't talk much because Sunny and the girls were there too. Does Bennett know?"

"Meredith made Amelie promise to let bygones be bygones. I wonder how he'll take the news."

"I wonder if Bennett will *get* the news," Mela replied. "What about you? Do you want to see your brother?"

A cotton-puff cloud drifted across the sun before Peter answered. "If nothing else, I'd like to see with my own eyes he's alive."

"I think that's a good idea. Family is important. Even if it isn't the reunion you hope for—at least you two get to talk. Things will become clear. Who knows, maybe there's even a second chance to connect. I know I used to like Charlie. A lot."

Before, Peter would've raised an eyebrow at Mela saying she'd liked him. Now, he simply said, "I used to like Charlie too."

CHAPTER 19

The nurse checked her clipboard. "Sunny June Gardener?"

"Gardiner. Here." Mela stood and helped Sunny get up. The revelation about Amelie and Charlie was still spinning in her head, but she needed to focus on her aunt.

"This is it." Mela squeezed Sunny's arm. "We're going to get the green light for the surgery today. I can feel it. You're as skinny as a matchstick."

"Don't know about that." Sunny tugged her blouse over her belly.

It had shrunk, though. Mela didn't have a scale at home, but she could see the difference. "Come on, let's do this," she whispered, guiding Sunny through the doors the nurse opened.

"He'll be right in," the nurse said. "If you could step on the scale for me?" Without commenting, she weighed Sunny and took her blood pressure, then tapped her info into the computer and left.

Mela settled Sunny in a chair, and before long, the doctor appeared.

"Hello again," he said, busily checking his tablet. "How are you?"

"Good," Sunny mumbled. Her fingers tightened around Mela's hand.

"Good. Hmm...good, good, good." He looked up with a smile. "I asked you to lose fifteen pounds, and you did. Well done! What was your secret?" He seemed genuinely pleased.

"My family," Sunny said. She looked surprised. "They starved me."

Mela shook her head at the doctor. "No processed foods," she said. "Lots of veggies and lean protein and a sprinkle of treats. That's all it took."

The doctor chuckled, swiping on his tablet. "Blood pressure down, sugar was already good last time... Looks like the next step is scheduling. Do you want to go ahead?"

Sunny inhaled.

Mela raised an eyebrow.

"Well?" The doctor looked up. "Should we schedule? I recommend you go ahead. That joint is only going to get worse."

"Yes," Sunny said and swallowed audibly. "The sooner, the better."

"Do it before she runs," Mela teased.

"Great. Stay here, and someone will come and set you up." The doctor held out his hand, and both Sunny and Mela shook. "See you soon!"

He left, and the nurse came back. "I'm so happy for you," she said. "My dad just went through knee surgery.

It's more complicated, but he's doing great. So let's see. Hmmm." She studied the timetables on the screen. "Usually it takes a while to get a date. But we've had a couple of cancellations, so maybe we can get you in a little early." She pointed at Sunny. "You don't take any medications, correct? How about aspirin? Vitamins?"

"Only vegetables and sunshine," Sunny said nervously.

"We can fit you in next week since you're cleared." The nurse beamed at Mela. "Can you do that?"

"Yes." Mela pressed Sunny's hand. "We can do that."

The nurse gave Sunny instructions, tapped on the keyboard and double-checked the date and time with Mela, then printed out a few sheets and handed them to Sunny together with an appointment card. "Any other questions?"

"We're good," Mela said when Sunny didn't answer. "Thank you."

"You're all set." The nurse stood. "We'll see you in a week." She left.

Mela gathered their purses. "You okay, Sunny?"

"I can't believe it's going to happen," Sunny replied. "What if something goes wrong?"

"What if it works out?" Mela took Sunny's arm and led her out of the building. "What if you trust the surgery will go great and you'll get back your ability to walk and do what you love? Why not choose those thoughts instead?"

They made their way out of the building and into the parking elevator.

"But what if..." Sunny whispered.

"You're in great shape and have every reason to expect it will go well," Mela said earnestly. "The odds are in your favor. But this is your choice. You don't have to do it."

Sunny's expression turned from fear to hope to resignation. The elevator doors opened, and she began the painful limp across the parking lot. Mela helped her into the passenger seat. "Don't be so reasonable," Sunny complained. "I need you to be scared with me."

Mela shook her head. "You just want me to keep talking you into it. But that's a thankless job and also not my responsibility. Make up your own mind, auntie."

Sunny strapped herself in. "Ah," she said when Mela pulled out of the parking lot. "You're right. I've made up my mind."

"I'm well aware," Mela said sweetly. "Listen, why don't we go celebrate?"

"Celebrate how? I'll have you know that losing this weight wasn't easy."

"We can have a lobster roll on the seawall. You still need to eat *something*."

"I'd love to see the seawall," Sunny said. "It's been years."

Mela flicked her blinker and turned down a small street lined with feathery fir trees. At the end was the seawall, a place where the natural shore had been fortified with rocks to protect the land from the waves. Halfway between Sandville and Bay Harbor, it was a famous tourist spot. Even people from Bay Port would make a trip out here to buy lobster, oyster, and clam meals at the famous Seafood Shack and admire the rock pools.

When Mela parked, it was almost empty. Only a lone woman was sitting on the seawall, her back to the parking lot, looking out at the ocean.

There was something familiar about her.

Sunny squinted. "Is that Johanna?"

"Johanna?"

Johanna used to be Mela's assistant. After Mela's divorce, the young woman had decided to follow to Bay Harbor, where she quickly made friends and helped Sunny retrieve some of her belongings. She'd meant to settle permanently—and even went so far as to look at houses with a real estate agent—when a family emergency called her home.

Mela hadn't heard from Johanna since.

"Can you make it to the tables?" she asked Sunny, handing her the crutch she kept in the car. Sunny took it and set off for the picnic benches by the Shack.

Mela crossed the parking lot. "Johanna?" she called out when she got closer to the woman. "Is that you?"

The woman looked over her shoulder. Large sunglasses shaded her eyes, but Mela recognized her immediately.

"Mela." Johanna swung her legs back over the wall and pushed her dark glasses up. "How are you?"

"I'm good, Johanna," she said. "More to the point, how are you? I was worried when I didn't hear back from you."

Johanna pushed her hands into the pockets of her jeans. "My mom passed away," she said quietly. "I feel pretty rough. I'm barely starting to understand it's real."

"I'm so sorry, honey. Can I hug you?"

Johanna stood and opened her arms, and Mela gave her a long hug.

When Mela returned to Bay Harbor, the accident that took her own mother's life and all the grief that came with it had come up again. Everyone grieved in their way, but it helped to have friends.

"Would you like to eat with Sunny and me?" Mela asked.

"Sunny is here?" Johanna liked the old woman—and Sunny adored her right back.

"Yes, she's sitting at the table over there." Mela pointed, and Sunny waved. "Come on, let's go say hi."

Together, they went to the outside seating area.

"Sunny," Johanna said and hugged Sunny too.

Sunny squinted at her. "Why do you look so sad, hon?"

"My mom passed away. We expected it, but it's rough."

"Oh no. I'm so sorry." Sunny patted the seat beside her. "Sit with us, my dear."

"Are you back in Bay Harbor for good?" Mela handed everyone a menu.

"If I can find a place to stay. I was counting on the motel, but it's not open."

"Peter is renovating, though I'm sure he can find a room for you. You can also always stay with me. I have room because Kimmie just got the keys to her own house."

"Oh, she moved in?" Johanna looked up. "That girl... I'll still be jotting down pros and cons by the time she's flipped her house and sells at a profit."

Mela smiled. "Kimmie likes a fast pace. But so do you. I'm sure you can find a place if you still want to live here."

The owner of the Shack wore an apron and a fedora hat when he came out. "Have you ladies decided?"

"Lobster rolls for everyone," Mela declared. "Johanna, you like lobster, don't you?" The young woman looked too skinny for her taste. If the energy was off, the slimmest waist in the world couldn't make up for it.

Johanna nodded, and the owner went back to cook up the order. "I'd love to stay a few days," Johanna admitted. "If it's no bother."

"It's no bother," Mela promised.

"I'll have my hip replaced next week," Sunny announced.

"My mom's friend went through that a while ago." Johanna smiled. "If you like, I can help you during the recovery. It takes a while, you know."

"I could hire you for a few months to help out," Mela said suddenly. "What do you think?"

Johanna looked at Sunny. "Would you be comfortable with that?"

Sunny nodded. "It would be a relief, to be honest. Mela can't do everything."

"Then I'd love that, Mela," Johanna said gratefully. "It would give me time to find work as a virtual assistant and set up shop. I haven't looked as hard as I should have. You can pay me by letting me stay in the house."

"Staying in the house is free," Mela declared. "You were already invited as a friend. I'm happy to pay, but we can talk about the details later. For now...I see some yummy big plates coming our way!"

Soon, they were busy eating warm rolls stuffed with chunks of lobster meat, creamy coleslaw, and crisp french fries hot from the fryer.

"This is such a treat," Sunny announced and dipped her last fry into a bit of lobster mayonnaise. "Though I think I had better not come back so soon."

"I haven't eaten this much in... I don't know. Weeks," Johanna said. She sounded more cheerful than before, and she had cleared her food.

"Do you have a car?" Mela asked.

"I do. I'm parked behind the shack."

"Are you going to drive to Bay Harbor now?"

Johanna sighed. "I just... Can I come tomorrow morning? I still have a few things to do."

"Sure. Take your time. We'll see you at home."

"12 Seasweet Lane," Johanna confirmed. "I'll catch up with you. And Mela—thank you. Once again."

Mela looked at her searchingly. "We're counting on seeing you soon, okay?"

"Okay."

Johanna was still sitting by the time Mela had brought Sunny back to the car and turned to wave.

She waved back.

"I hope she's all right," Sunny said when Mela started the car. "I wish she'd come with us. Something makes me want to keep an eye on her."

Mela nodded. "I feel the same," she said. "I hope she'll show up tomorrow."

CHAPTER 20

Amelie tugged a short curl over her ear, then pushed it back again. She turned in front of the bathroom mirror, deciding she didn't look half bad. Her favorite lemon-yellow dress hugged her curves just so, and the color brightened her skin. She weighed more than she liked—she'd been a skinny kid, but that changed in her teen years.

Her body issues stemmed of course from Meredith, who was always dieting herself, and who to this day praised Amelie when she was slim but pointedly withheld praise whenever she gained weight. Mela had helped her over her swimsuit hang-up by not taking no for an answer. Even a therapist needed a good friend to boost their confidence. Amelie tugged the dress lower.

The doorbell rang, and her heart skipped a beat. She pressed a hand to her chest. How long had she waited for this moment?

Every minute of every day since she found the blue line on the pregnancy test, it suddenly seemed. She'd always wanted to tell Charlie. Only, she couldn't. But now was the big moment. The big reveal, thirty years delayed.

"It's okay," she whispered at her reflection. "Whatever his reaction is going to be, it's okay." She slipped on her sandals and went downstairs.

Telling Charlie wasn't the problem.

Telling Bennett was another thing.

Amelie knew he wouldn't overreact; her son had never overreacted once in his life. He wouldn't be mad at her for waiting so long to tell him, either. Probably.

Hopefully, he wasn't too stressed from moving to Bay Harbor. At the moment, he was making lots of short, quick trips back and forth between here and Cape Bass.

Excited and nervous, Amelie's thoughts fluttered to her son's move. Every time he visited, he brought more boxes to fill the guest rooms upstairs. The basement was already crammed full. They'd have to rent a storage unit before Meredith came—Meredith and the moving truck full of her things.

She had reached the front door. She took a quick, deep breath and opened it.

There stood Charlie, holding a bouquet of delphinium and roses, snapdragons and asters. His jaw relaxed when he saw her. "Hi. For a moment, I thought you weren't going to open."

She smiled and pointed over her shoulder. "I was only upstairs."

In the hours between their first conversation and that evening, she had become more and more convinced Charlie really did write a letter and Dad snatched it.

It would explain so many things. Like Dad storming up to the motel and engaging in a yelling match with Charlie's dad before Amelie even discovered she was pregnant. It had always seemed an overreaction to finding out his daughter had gone to prom with the wrong boy.

Charlie cleared his throat. "These are for you," he said and filled her arms with colorful bounty.

"It's beautiful, Charlie. Come inside, I'll just put them in a vase."

He hesitated for a moment. "I don't want to disturb anyone."

Her thoughts flew to Bennett, but Bennett was on his way to Cape Bass; he'd left right after learning how to change a baby's diaper.

"I'm alone," she told Charlie and opened the door wider.

He stepped inside. He was dressed in jeans and a blue button-down shirt with folded sleeves.

"Well—still the same house," she remarked lightly as she led the way to the kitchen. She pulled a vase from the cabinet and filled it with water, then arranged the flowers.

"Never in my life did I think I'd see the inside," Charlie admitted with a tight laugh.

"I was *strictly* forbidden to date you," Amelie agreed. "Having you in here after all these years feels pretty strange."

"I agree," he murmured, letting his gaze wander. "It looks completely different than I expected."

"Does it? How?" Amelie put a hand on her hip. Like with the geraniums, she hadn't changed much. A touch-up here and there, that was it. The discussion she had with Mom over painting the cherry cabinets lasted six months and only ended when Amelie was too fed up with wasting any more time on cabinet doors. They stayed a dull red, forever clashing with the bright geraniums in front of the window.

"I don't know how it's different," Charlie said. "I didn't have a particular look in mind. It's just not what I expected. But it's beautiful, of course." There was an insincere wobble in his words.

"Hmm." The thought of the house she'd looked at with the real estate agent flashed through Amelie's mind. Charlie's voice wouldn't waver if he saw how pretty and bright that kitchen was. But it didn't matter. "Should we leave?" she asked, putting the vase on the kitchen island. The pastel colors would look much prettier in the other kitchen.

"Where would you like to go?"

"There aren't so many options. The only restaurants in driving distance are the Seawall Shack, the Beach Bistro, and a small coffee place near the Harbor."

"No restaurants?" He looked surprised.

"Not really. We don't get tourists since Bay Port and Sandville ramped up their efforts to attract them."

"Well, maybe that's for the best," Charlie murmured. "What happened to the motel?"

Amelie tilted her head. "Peter lives there. Have you not stopped by?"

Charlie frowned. "I passed it—but it looked derelict, with a trash dumpster out front. I didn't even know Peter lives in Bay Harbor. Last time I searched the internet, I got the impression he lived in Africa and was doing research. Tanzania, wasn't it? The Serengeti?"

"Peter came back years ago, Charlie. He took over the motel after your dad passed away, and he's renovating it. Hence the dumpster."

"I had no idea." The corners of Charlie's mouth dropped in surprise.

"Why did you never contact him, Charlie?" Or her?

"I tried a few years ago. I emailed a university address I found but never heard back. I thought he wasn't interested. Or maybe he'd moved already, and the email address was old. I didn't have anything else to follow up."

"You aren't on the internet."

He tilted his head. "You looked for me?"

"I might've." She shrugged.

After a moment, he said, "You're not to be found either."

"I try to stay away." Even her social media accounts didn't show her full name. "We like our privacy, don't we?"

"For better or worse," he agreed. "Listen, do I remember seeing a pizzeria somewhere?"

"Oh. It's so new it slipped my mind. Let's go there; I'm glad you thought of it."

This time, they drove together in Charlie's rental car to the tiny pizzeria that had opened in Bay Harbor. It was run by Laurel, sister to Amelie's real estate agent Kelly.

After they exchanged greetings, Laurel showed them to a table on the sidewalk. It was a perfect spot for a cozy restaurant—the street was used more by pedestrians than cars since it was made from bumpy cobblestones and only led to the marketplace.

They sat, and Laurel brought water and menus to the table. "Kelly was telling me about the house she showed you. It sounds like you fell in love with it." She smiled. "So are you going to buy it?"

CHAPTER 21

"I honestly wish I could," Amelie said and pulled a face at how sincere she sounded. "But I'm just not able to. I adore the house, though. I didn't know we had places like that in Bay Harbor."

"What house is that?" Charlie asked, and Laurel told him about the house on Meadow Drive.

It reminded Amelie that Meredith was moving back to Bay Harbor. It made selling the old family home impossible, and without that sale, there'd never be money for a down payment.

"Amelie? Would you like a glass of wine?"

Both Laurel and Charlie were looking at her.

"Sorry. I'll just have iced tea," Amelie said.

"The same for me, please." Charlie nodded at Laurel.

"Back in a sec." She disappeared.

Amelie studied the menu. "I'll have p pizza," she decided. "That sounds nice."

"My eye is on the pear and bacon pizza," Charlie said and glanced over his menu card at Amelie. "And maybe an appetizer?"

"Or a dessert. I hear Laurel's tiramisu is out of this world," Amelie said. "I tried my hand at tiramisu, so I'd like to see what she did there."

When Laurel came back with the iced tea, they put in their orders, and Charlie also asked for an appetizer sampler.

"So," he said when they were alone again—almost alone. The neighboring tables were filling as well, but everybody was engaged in their quiet conversations. "I told you the deepest darkest secrets of my past, Amelie. How about you? How have you been since we last saw each other? I was convinced you would marry and have a house full of kids."

"About that." Amelie dabbed the corners of her mouth with her napkin and took a sip from her glass. Her mouth was dry. "Let's go back to prom night. You, um...remember what happened."

Charlie folded his hands. "I never forgot."

"So, yes." Suddenly, Amelie had no idea how to say it. "For me, Charlie, the magic didn't stop at midnight."

His eyes were earnest. "Nor for me, Amelie. I mean it when I say I never forgot."

"No." Amelie cleared her throat. "I mean, I never forgot either, though there were plenty of times I wished I could. But I couldn't. I *couldn't* turn the clock back."

He frowned. "Did you want to?"

Amelie sighed. "For nine months, Charlie, I wanted nothing more. And then, after that ninth month, I was too sleep-deprived to do much wanting."

His gaze turned first inward, and then his eyes closed. "Nine months, Amelie?"

"Yes," she replied. "That's how long it takes to carry the consequences. Quite literally."

Charlie covered his face before dropping his hands again. "Are you serious, Amelie? Don't mess with me, please. I can't...?"

"Yes, I'm serious." Amelie tapped a finger on the table to underline her words. "His name is Bennett, he's a homicide detective in Cape Bass, and he'll turn thirty-one in September. And, Charlie..." She leaned forward. "He's the best thing that happened in my life. I mean it."

Charlie looked dazed. "Are you *sure* I'm..."

Amelie gave him a frosty look. "You of all people don't want to ask me that, Charles Townson. Bennett was almost ten before I even *thought* about dating again."

"Bennett," Charlie said slowly. "You called him Bennett after Mom's dad."

Amelie nodded. "I remembered how much you liked your grandpa. I couldn't tell you about your son, but I wanted..." She looked at her hands. "I was angry at you, but I'm also a sentimental fool."

"I...don't know what to say."

Just then, Laurel appeared with a large platter of appetizers. Mela spotted smoked salmon crostini and bacon-wrapped prunes, jalapeño poppers, and tiny baked Bries with sliced figs and cranberry sauce. But her appetite was gone.

"Bon appétit." Laurel left, and they sat silently, looking at each other.

Finally, Charlie stirred. "That can't have been easy for you."

"No," Amelie said emphatically. "It wasn't. Having that letter you mentioned would have helped a lot."

He closed his eyes as if hurt by the implied suspicion. "I did leave that letter," he said. "I swear, Amelie."

She nodded but didn't reply. There was nothing to say.

"If you *had* gotten it," Charlie said. "Would you have told me?"

She looked up, surprised. "The letter said how to get in touch?"

"I put my address in it," Charlie said. "Or at least what I hoped it would be."

"What address?"

"A cattle ranch," he replied. "In Australia. I read about it in a National Geographic magazine at school; the article said they were short on farm hands. I figured Dad would never find me there."

"You went to Australia?" Amelie couldn't believe it.

"Once I wrote it in that letter, I had to. So you would know where I was." He scrunched his napkin into a ball. "I was sure I'd have a reply from you waiting for me when I arrived a few weeks later. When I didn't, I figured you were grounded and couldn't send a letter. Then I figured you were mad. And on it went, my list of reasons why you didn't write back."

He met her eye. "I wasn't going to talk about it because it was a dark chapter for me. But I sent you another letter. And another. I was going to write until I heard from you, Amelie."

"What?" She stared at him, shocked.

"For a year, I wrote to you every two weeks. I sent twenty-four letters after that first one, Amelie."

"Twenty-five letters?"

His eyes narrowed. "You didn't get a single one?"

"No, Charlie. I never got a single letter." Amelie was lost for words.

He picked up a smoked salmon crostino, studied it, and then set it on his plate as if it was a rock, not a savory morsel. "I worked on that ranch for ten years, and every day I waited to hear from you." He smiled wistfully. "Until my hope became as dusty as my boots. I finally figured you forgot about me."

"I was waiting until I finally gave up too. I couldn't wait any longer. I had to be there for Bennett." They'd both waited ten years... She looked up, and their eyes met.

"I wish I had known. I wish I had known you were waiting too," he said softly.

"Oh, Charlie. Why didn't you *call*?"

"Your parents always answered the phone, remember?" He spread his hands. "It was long before the internet and cell phones came to the outback, Amelie. We used ham radios on the ranch, and those didn't work half the time. The nearest phone that could do international calls was a day's drive away. And when

I finally had my own phone, your number had been disconnected."

Amelie covered her mouth with a hand. To think of Charlie rounding cattle in the heat, listening to insects singing in the bush, waiting to hear from her...

"It's okay, Amelie," Charlie said and held out a hand. His fingers trembled. "We had good lives, no? We made the best of it."

They had been so young. Only teens. She put her hand in his. "Yes, we did." But she couldn't help thinking. What would have happened had she known he was in Australia? Would she have gone to him? She would have wanted to. But she wouldn't have been brave enough to leave Bay Harbor and her family. It took more than a heartfelt letter to raise a baby in the bush.

Amelie relaxed into her chair, pulling her hand from his. "Charlie," she said. "I will find out what happened to your letters. If they still exist, I will find them, and then I will read every single one, and I will write you back."

"And I have a son," he said, slowly tasting each word. "My son Bennett."

"He doesn't know about you," Amelie warned. "I didn't tell him."

His face stilled. "Why not?"

"Because I thought you had left me without a word."

"You were angry while I waited for your letter. We were living different truths because of a...a stupid mistake." He ran his fingers through his hair.

"Even if we had been together, living the same truth, it would have been a mistake. We were too young, Charlie."

"How young is too young, Amelie?" Charlie looked up. "How do you know it would have been wrong?"

"There are always different paths," she said. "We only get to choose one."

"And you'd have chosen to stay?" He smiled, but there was sadness in the shape of his mouth.

"I don't know, honestly. What would I have done with a baby in the Australian bush? I was unhappy here, but it was safe. I could take care of my son. Mom helped, so I was able to go to college. I don't know, Charlie. It wasn't easy, but maybe it was for the best."

He nodded his understanding but didn't reply.

"I will tell Bennett about you tomorrow," Amelie promised. "He's coming back to Bay Harbor."

"Can I see him?"

"He's a grown man, Charlie. You don't have to ask me."

"I'm asking you, Amelie."

"See him. Speak with him. You'll be glad you did."

"Thank you."

"I think I lost my appetite. It doesn't seem right to eat jalapeños stuffed with cream cheese and bacon." She smiled an apology.

"I agree." He rose. "I'll ask the young lady to give the food to someone else. Maybe we can go walk along the water instead."

The sun was sinking, tinting the sky golden and red; the air was warm, and it smelled of dry dune sand and ebbing sea. "I'd like that," Amelie said. "There's still so much I want to ask."

"I'll only be a moment. Wait for me." He raised a single eyebrow. "*Wait* for me, Amelie."

She smiled back; he could still make her laugh. "I promise, Charlie. I'll wait right here. Don't leave without me."

CHAPTER 22

Amelie slipped off her sandals to feel the sand under her feet. Here, near the harbor, the beach was littered with small pebbles and shells, bits of driftwood, and the eventual stranded jellyfish or sea urchin. She liked it the way she liked all beaches. Those with fine sand were great for swimming. Wild beaches were good for finding shells and milky sea glass. This beach was one of the best for walking. The ground was firm enough to carry, and there was a sprinkle of treasure to draw the eye. Like background music at a party, scanning for pretty shells kept silences from becoming awkward.

And it was a little awkward to walk with Charlie beside her. It was awkward to feel the way Amelie felt—still, again—about him. She had trained herself to believe he callously broke her teenage heart. And now it seemed—maybe, possibly—she'd been wrong.

Now it seemed as if Charlie had loved her. As much as she'd loved him.

Maybe more.

Where did they stand now? Every few moments, she became more aware of his presence, the still-familiar face, the fact that he was her son's father. Every few moments, Amelie felt the urge to touch Charlie's arm. Or his hand. Or his face—to trail her fingers along his jaw and cheek, to get to know again how he felt.

But familiar as Charlie seemed, he was a stranger now.

Risking what harmony and calm she'd created in her life seemed...stupid.

"Charlie?" she asked.

"Yes?" He looked at her. His bright-blue eyes could still make her breath hitch.

Peter had looked at her a thousand times with the same eyes, and her breath never hitched. It wasn't the color or the shape. It was the spirit behind the eyes that attracted her.

"Do you still live in Australia?" she asked. "Are you still a ranch hand?"

The corners of his eyes crinkled. "I still live in Australia. But it's been a long time since I was a ranch hand."

Amelie's heart constricted. Australia was impossibly far away. "What do you do now?"

"I own my own ranch."

"Tell me about it," Amelie said. She stopped to pick up a pretty sand dollar that was white and perfectly intact.

"I'll carry it for you," Charlie offered. Amelie handed him the sand dollar with a smile. Maybe Bennett's gentlemanly manners were due to his genes, not her efforts.

"It's a cattle ranch," Charlie said. "They roam free, and my cowboys take care of them." He chuckled at his description. "It's more complicated than that. But in a nutshell."

"Do you live on the ranch?"

"I did for about fifteen years. But I missed the sea." He smiled. "And people. Other people than my cowboy crew, I mean. So I bought a place in Sydney."

"Do you like Sydney?"

He nodded. "I love it. I love the ranch too. The wilderness and the freedom you feel when you're there."

"And do you have a partner?" Amelie picked up a piece of blue sea glass, washed it off, and handed it to Charlie. "You said you don't have kids. Other than your firstborn, I mean."

"Huh." Charlie exhaled. "It will take a while to get used to having a firstborn." He stopped and looked up at the sky that had turned from burnished gold to velvety plum. His jaw stiffened.

Amelie threw caution to the wind and reached out after all to touch his arm. "It's okay," she said softly. "It's all right."

"I dreamed of being the perfect dad," Charlie murmured and continued walking. "I meant to be so good to my children. I meant to be the dad I wished I had."

"Did you?" Amelie looked out at the darkening sea. Far out, the waves wore white crests that shimmered in the fading evening light and disappeared. What a day this had been. "Everything I thought about you was wrong. I thought you ran from me."

It took him a while to respond.

"What about you, Amelie?" he finally asked, studying her treasures in his hand. "Would you have stuck to a boy from the wrong side of the tracks?"

She shook her head. "I told you before you weren't on the wrong side of the tracks. You lived a few minutes down the road from me."

"But would you have—" He took a breath that widened his chest. "Would you have married me if I'd asked?"

It was Amelie's turn to fall quiet.

She'd dreamed her teenage dreams like any other girl. She'd wanted to walk down the aisle in a mermaid gown and have calla lilies and fairy lights.

"Your parents hated me," Charlie reminded her. "Your dad took my letters so you wouldn't see them. Do you think you would have wanted to marry me? Me, with my alcoholic dad, no job prospects, and barely out of high school?"

Amelie turned to meet his eyes. "Yes," she said defiantly. "I would have married you. That's exactly why my dad hid the letters. He didn't want me to know how to get in touch with you."

Charlie pressed his lips together. "Then that makes it harder," he murmured. "If I had stood up to my father and stayed, I could have had you and my son."

"What happened, happened," Amelie said automatically. "Let's not think about all the what-ifs." As if it was that easy...

For a while they walked on, their silhouettes blurring as night settled over the beach.

"See the star?" Charlie pointed at the sky.

"Where?"

He stopped walking and put his face close to hers to see what she saw. "Right there." He pointed again.

Amelie saw the star. It was as faint as Charlie's breath brushing her neck. His scent hugged her, warm and dry and woody like beach heather on a sunny day in fall. "We should go back. The tide is going to turn and flood the beach."

"Is it getting too hazardous for you?" he murmured.

"Yes." Amelie shivered and took a few steps away from him. "It is, actually."

He gestured back from where they'd come. "After you, Amelie. I'll follow wherever you go."

"Oh, stop it," she said, but then she had to laugh, and the sea rushed a melody that washed away any awkwardness.

They were almost at the boardwalk when two figures materialized in the dark ahead.

Amelie squinted. "Those two look familiar."

Charlie slowed, but the figures came closer nevertheless. "Peter?" Charlie asked. "*Mela?*"

"Hello, Charlie." Mela held Peter's hand.

Peter stared at his younger brother, and for a moment, Amelie was scared Peter would run, or fight, or do something that matched the expression on his face. Instead, he stepped forward and pulled Charlie into a hug.

Mela came over and slipped her arm under Amelie's. "I made Peter tell me about Charlie and you," she whispered. "Don't be angry."

Amelie looked at her friend. She no longer had to keep a secret. A mismatched thread weaving through her life was finally cut.

"Did you tell Bennett?"

"Not yet." Amelie inhaled the night air, looking out at the black sea and not seeing anything. "But I'll have to do it soon."

CHAPTER 23

"Bennett?" Nervously, Amelie pressed her cell phone to her ear. She was sitting in Mela's living room. Night had fallen, as heavy and dark and soft as a fur blanket. Mela and the Townson brothers sat on the patio in the glow of citronella lanterns and torches. The rest of the family was tucked into bed, Kimmie in her new house.

"Are you okay?" Bennett sounded alarmed. The white noise rushing in the background told Amelie he was driving.

"Yes, I'm okay. Are you still working?"

"I'm not. I got official word that I'm hired in Bay Harbor, Mom. I'm almost there. I decided to leave tonight instead of tomorrow morning. It was supposed to be a surprise, but I guess now you know."

"Oh. Um." Amelie hadn't expected her son back so soon. "Bennett, I have to tell you something. I didn't mean to do it on the phone, but things moved fast, and I'd like you to know."

"You're scaring me," he said, using his stern detective voice. "Tell me what's going on, please."

"Everything's good. I don't... I'm at Mela's. Can you come here?"

"Yes. Why? I don't like suspense."

Amelie closed her eyes. "Your father is here, Bennett."

"My—my what? What did you say?"

"Your father is in Bay Harbor."

Bennett groaned. "Mom, my *father*? Are you serious?"

"Yes, I'm serious."

"Well...so after years of not mentioning him, you suddenly want me to meet him?"

"It's up to you, of course. I'd like it if you came, but it is your choice. Bennett, I honestly thought I'd never see him again. I never thought he wanted me—or you. I'm just now learning that his story might be different from what I thought. Will you come?"

"Tonight? I mean, how long is he here?"

"He lives in Sydney, Australia. There's so much to— I don't know much more. But I want to tell you who he is."

"Charlie Townson," Bennett said.

"What? How did you know?" Amelie's eyes flew open.

He chuckled. "Sweet mother, I'm a detective. It took very little to put it together."

"Bennett," Amelie said weakly. "I don't know where to start with you."

"Same," Bennett said, and then the connection crackled and fizzed. "Listen, Mom, I'm driving past Beach Cove right now, and we'll lose the call. Are you still going to be at Mela's in an hour?"

"I think we might be here all night," Amelie said. "Peter is here too, and he and Charlie are catching up."

"And are you all right?"

Amelie sighed. "I'm all right. How are you?"

"Surprised he came," Bennett said dryly. "I'll come to say hi, but don't expect me to call him papa."

"No, of course not." Amelie had to laugh. "Thank you, Bennett. I love you more than life and I can't wait to see you."

The connection fizzled again, and then it was gone. Amelie put her head in her hands.

Bennett had known all along. What else was he hiding behind those dark eyes?

Amelie went back out to join the others. The citronella torches glowed in the still night air, and the velvety black of flower beds and bushes flickered with the fairy lights of fireflies.

Charlie was telling the story of how he left the motel after his father cracked his ribs. Peter was sitting beside Mela, listening without interrupting. But when Charlie finished, he stirred. "Charlie, I wish you'd told me," he said. "I wish I had known what was happening after I left."

"You had barely gotten out yourself. I wasn't going to let you take care of me," Charlie said. Both brothers looked tense, the set of their shoulders the same, their faces tight.

Amelie slipped quietly back into her chair. The more the brothers talked, the better. But both men noticed, turning to look at her.

"When do you fly back to Australia, Charlie?" Amelie asked.

He blew out a breath. "I left the date flexible because I thought I'd play this visit by ear."

"So there is time to talk about everything." She nodded at Peter. "It will take time to adjust. We don't have to solve all the riddles and feel all the feelings right now. It's too much for one night."

"Are you counseling us, Amelie?" Peter grinned.

"I wouldn't dare."

"Right." Peter leaned back. "Charlie, I took over the motel after Dad died. I've renovated a few of the rooms, and you're welcome to stay there."

"Oh. Thanks. That's unexpected, Peter, I didn't mean to... I do have a place to stay."

"Maybe you should make new memories of the place," Amelie encouraged him.

Charlie's eyes glinted in the flickering light when he looked at her. "You're right. Peter, thanks, my brother. I appreciate it." He squared his shoulders. "I appreciate all you have done for Amelie—and my son."

"That's me, I guess," came a deep voice from the dark living room, and then Bennett stepped out on the patio.

"Bennett!" Amelie stood and went to him. He felt like a rock when she put her hand on his arm. "Bennett, this is Charlie. Charles. Charles Townson."

Her heart was drumming a new rhythm in her chest as Bennett locked eyes with his father.

"I can see the resemblance," Mela said into the quiet, and everyone looked at her.

"Me too." Amelie clutched her hands. "Mela?"

"Yes, my dear?"

"Do you have coffee and maybe something sweet for us?"

"Of course I do." Mela rose. "Sunny made a peach cobbler, and I have maple-pecan ice cream to go with it. Good?" Without waiting for a response, she and Peter went inside.

"Bennett." Charlie stood and went to him. He held out a hand. "I'm glad I get to meet you."

Bennett looked at the hand and then at Amelie, who couldn't breathe, and then he opened his arms and hugged Charlie. Charlie stiffened at first but wasn't long to hug Bennett back.

"Good to see you, Dad," Bennett said when he let go.

Amelie's eyes widened.

"Mom, if you look this happy about having him here, I'm all right calling him dad." Bennett came and hugged her too.

Amelie looked at Charlie. His eyes were shiny. "Sit down, you two," she said with what little air she had to spare. "Charlie, if you don't mind, would you tell Bennett what happened back then?"

"I will."

The men sat.

"Mela, you and Peter should join us," Amelie said when her friend returned with coffee and plates of cobbler and ice cream she set before them.

"You are a good uncle," Bennett said to Peter. "You're always there when I need you."

The corners of Peter's lips trembled. Then he cleared his throat. "I did my best, kid."

"I know. Thank you." Bennett crossed his arms in front of his chest, and Charlie told his story for the third time.

And that, Amelie decided when he was done, was enough.

The past was the past.

She looked at the faces around the table. They were one family. And they were all doing the best they could.

It was time for a new beginning.

CHAPTER 24

Kimmie hitched up the legs of her denim overalls and perched on the stone wall in the garden. Then she tore off a piece of her chocolate croissant and dipped it into the steaming hot cocoa that smelled like the answer to all questions. She didn't usually have much of a sweet tooth, but today she felt like comfort food for breakfast. Early as it was, the morning had already been eventful, with both a brand-new family addition and Johanna suddenly showing up.

Plus, the night in her new house had been...spooky. Twice, she'd woken and thought someone was standing at the door, only to jump up and find it was a moon shadow.

Across Mom's patio table, Sisley was still laughing about that, covering her mouth as if that would hide her glee at her elder sister's weakness.

Tired as she was, Kimmie grinned. "I can see you laughing," she said. "Johanna, tell her to take my shadows seriously."

Johanna glumly folded her napkin. "It worries me that you're seeing scary things. With your work and all, you have to be on the lookout for PTSD."

Kimmie put her croissant down. She'd come to like Johanna. They were the same age, and both had straightforward, adventurous natures. As Mom's former assistant, Johanna even knew pretty much everything about the family.

Usually, Jo was bubbly and happy. But she'd come back from her mom's funeral somber and sad.

Kimmie wished she could help somehow. Of course, she couldn't. There was probably nothing anyone could do to make it better other than behaving fairly normally around Johanna and not shying away from her dark mood.

"It's not PTSD," Kimmie declared mildly. "Just the moon shining through an old willow tree into the house. I'll get blinds."

The monitor blinked and crackled. Sisley stood. "Sounds like Lovie woke up. See you later." She tightened the belt of her robe, picked up her cup of Earl Grey, and went inside.

Out of habit from working in dangerous areas, Kimmie took stock of where everyone was while she finished her breakfast.

Sunny was clanging pots in the kitchen. She was in a proper cooking frenzy now the surgery was scheduled.

Mom, Peter, Amelie, and the man Charlie who had turned out to be both Peter's brother and Bennett's dad were making honey in the barn, working to empty the frames so they could put them back in the hives. The honey extractor hummed in the background, vying with the rushing sea for most wholesome white noise.

"How are you, Johanna?" Kimmie blew into the mug to cool the cocoa. "Is there anything you'd like to do?"

Johanna pushed a toast crumb around her plate. "I feel like I want to do something stupid just so I can feel something. I'm numb, and I don't like it."

"Don't do it," Kimmie warned. "Injuring yourself is not the answer."

"Then what is?"

Kimmie glanced at her. The woman had already gone into Sunny's house, which was in danger of slipping into the ocean at any moment. And that was Jo in a good mood. "Uh, let's do something nice. Something that will make you feel *better*, not give you a rush."

Johanna snipped the crumb off the table. "You're one to talk."

The front door creaked open and closed again. A moment later, Bennett appeared at the patio door.

"Good morning." He looked very handsome in his button-down shirt and jeans, hair still damp from the shower.

"Morning, Bennett," Kimmie said. "Come to join the honey-making fun? You know Johanna, don't you?"

"Yes, we've met. How are you?"

Johanna shook her head. "Reeling," she admitted and tried a smile. "Though it feels more like sinking into quicksand. My mother passed away. I knew it was coming, but it's hard."

"I'm so sorry." Bennett closed the door behind him and came to the table. "Can I do anything?"

She shook her head. "I just need a couple of weeks to process what happened."

Bennett hummed his agreement. "Kimmie, do you know where my mother is?"

"Everyone's in the barn," Kimmie said and set her mug down, balancing it on the uneven fieldstone wall.

"All of them?"

"Yeah. I hear you met your dad." She squinted at him against the morning sun. "Are you okay?"

Bennett folded up the sleeve of his shirt. "More than I thought I'd be. It's weird but good. At least I think it's good." He unrolled the sleeve again and started fresh.

"Sisley is upstairs, feeding the baby," Kimmie offered.

He patted the sleeve in place; it suddenly seemed to sit good enough. "Did Sisley catch any sleep?"

"She said she was up every hour to nurse, but Lovie was good in between."

"Great. Uh." He glanced at Johanna, who was looking out at the sea, and raised an eyebrow at Kimmie.

She shook her head—there was nothing they could do to help. Grief took its time.

Bennett nodded. "I better have a look at the honey shed." He left.

When Kimmie turned back to the table, Johanna lifted her head. "Does he like Sisley?" Johanna asked. "Like, like-like?"

"I'm pretty sure he does." Kimmie adjusted the slipping strap of her overalls. "For half a second there, I thought I had a crush on him myself. Maybe even for a full second. But embarrassing as it is to admit, he only had eyes for Sisley from the moment he met her." She sighed dramatically.

At least now Johanna's lips twitched into a small smile. "They'd make a cute couple."

Kimmie smiled back. "They would. The only drawback is it reminds me of how unlovable I am. I really messed up with Travis."

"All of us mess up all the time, Kimmie," Johanna said. "You know that. Accept yourself, warts and all."

Kimmie chuckled. "Sounds good. Only I can't seem to do it."

"Have you talked to him since the divorce?"

"I *should* have," Kimmie said. "Does that count?"

"I think you actually have to pick up the phone. Honestly, Kimmie, what's holding you back? You liked him enough to marry him, didn't you?"

"That doesn't matter anymore." Kimmie hopped off the wall, picked up the tray, and started stacking the breakfast things on it. "I just would like to know what went on in his head, you know?"

"Call him and ask." Johanna stood. "We don't have as much time as we think."

Kimmie stopped what she was doing and glanced at her friend. "Travis changed his number. Presumably so I'd leave him alone."

"He's probably as scared of explaining himself as you are of hearing him out. But come on. You're an investigator." Johanna took the teapot from Kimmie's hand. "What do you have to lose by reaching out?"

"Whatever's left of my pride, I guess." Kimmie sat back down. "But at least I'll know."

"Exactly." Johanna pushed Kimmie's cell toward her, set the teapot on the tray, and lifted it. "I'll go slam pots with Sunny in the kitchen."

"She's got a ton of cherries in the sink," Kimmie warned. "She's suddenly obsessed with tarts."

"If anything can cheer me up, it's pitting cherries. An activity both wholesome and useful."

"In that spirit, let me get the door for you." Kimmie went to pull the sliding door open, and Johanna disappeared with the tray.

Kimmie went back to the sun-warmed wall. Mom had planted more hydrangeas, and the pink and blue flower puffs swayed in the breeze. Kimmie pulled up her contacts; she still remembered the unknown number calling her. Some instinct had made her save it. She pressed redial before she could think about it. "Probably just spam," she whispered.

The phone rang a couple of times. Kimmie's thumb was ready to end the call when the line crackled.

"Yes?"

Kimmie inhaled. "It's Kimmie." She waited, grabbing a stone so hard her knuckles turned white.

There was a pause. "How did you get my number?"

"You called me. I saved the number because...well, I had a feeling it was you."

"Yeah. It was a mistake."

"Travis?" Kimmie needed to move to get rid of the tense energy. Pressing her phone to her ear, she swung her legs over the wall and started walking through the field toward the beach.

"Yes."

"Can we talk, please?"

There was a pause. Then he said, "Everything's settled. You made me sign the prenup and got the easy divorce it was meant for." The words were angry, but his voice wasn't.

"You know it was Dad who wanted the prenup. You were okay with it." Her father figured his assets would be his kids' someday, and he'd meant to protect both his money and children. Travis had agreed without twitching an eyelid. Kimmie couldn't believe that it had secretly hurt his feelings after all.

He didn't respond.

But he had called her. On some level or other, he wanted to talk too. Kimmie inhaled. "I'm not calling to fight, Travis. I don't want anything besides understanding what happened to us."

CHAPTER 25

Travis gave in with a sigh. "Okay. Maybe... Well, let's talk. Uh. Where are you?"

"I'm in Bay Harbor. It's a small town in Maine, by the sea. Right now, I'm walking to the beach." She let her palm graze the tops of the dry, sweet-smelling grass as she walked. "I just bought a house here."

"You bought a house in Maine? Why?"

"Because I wanted to." Kimmie picked a yellow daisy and twirled it between her fingers. "I love it here."

"You *love* it?"

She tucked the flower into the strap of her overalls. "Why wouldn't I? It's peaceful and slow and relaxing."

"You love your *job*," he said. "It's your one and only love, Kimmie."

She stopped where the grass and flowers ended, and sand started to replace soil. The sea lay ahead in sunny morning glory, and the air smelled of salt and kelp and the purple thistles that dotted the field.

"Is that why I found the divorce papers on my nightstand, Travis?" she asked. "Because I was doing my job?"

"You were busy."

"You were busy too," she said. "You never said it bothered you."

"It did."

Kimmie stepped out of her sandals and picked them up. "Well, I figured you'd say that was the reason," she said. "I wish we had talked about it, though. It seems like we could have fixed it. Maybe we could have both changed our schedules."

"Would you have worked less?"

"I would have thought about it." She stepped into the warm sand. "A *divorce* doesn't make a whole lot of sense if me working too much was all that bugged you. Besides, was it your expectation that I stay at home? Come on, it was not. You knew how much I traveled because you have the same job I do."

She sat, leaning against a bleached trunk of driftwood. "Travis?" she asked after a while. "Can you tell me what was really going on?"

"Okay. Kimmie...I didn't want to do this. Things weren't great; we never saw each other."

"So why didn't you say anything?"

He continued as if she hadn't spoken. "And then something happened. I couldn't deal with it."

Kimmie dug her fingers into the warm ground. "What happened?"

"Okay, this is going to be... I had a thing with a woman. An affair. A one-night stand."

She closed her eyes, trying not to react. It didn't matter because there was no marriage or relationship to save—the two of them were already divorced. She already knew he didn't want her anymore. "When?" she asked.

"It happened on my last assignment in Afghanistan."

Kimmie could barely hear what he was saying; she was so focused on staying centered. What had been his last assignment? There was only rushing in her head—rushing thoughts, rushing sounds filling her ears. "Who was it?" she blurted out.

"Just someone I was working with. She's... Her name's Tina Biltmore. She worked for us as a photographer."

Tina. Kimmie had never heard of her before.

"So you cheated on me," she stated. Divorced or not, it was hard to breathe. Kimmie was surprised she still cared so much. "Just trying to understand."

"My work in Afghanistan was over before we met, Kimmie," Travis said. "I didn't cheat on you. We didn't meet until later."

"What?" Kimmie shaded her eyes against the bright light dancing on the waves. "I don't understand. Wasn't your last girlfriend's name Katherine?"

He sighed. "Tina wasn't my girlfriend. I'd broken up with Kathy, I hadn't met you yet, and I was working in Afghanistan. It was one night, Kimmie. An accident. A real accident that neither one of us meant to happen. I wasn't proud of it, and I didn't feel like talking about it."

Kimmie breathed a little easier, but she knew she hadn't heard the end of the story yet. "Okay," she said. "So you liked her."

"She was great. I might've wanted more, but she wasn't interested. My ego took a hit, but it was my own fault for mixing personal stuff with business. She told me it'd been just for fun, I said fine. We left it at that.

"Okay." Kimmie pressed her lips together. How many more fun flings had her ex kept to himself?

"She went back to England as soon as she had taken her pictures. I met you soon after I got back and never thought about Tina again."

"So...I guess she came back?"

"In a way." Travis cleared his throat.

Kimmie wiped the sand off her hands and stood. She needed to move again. "Okay. Did you realize you still loved her or that I wasn't enough like her?"

It took him a while to answer. "It wasn't Tina getting back in touch, but a hospital. I was Tina's emergency contact."

"You were her emergency contact?" That made no sense, did it? It made no sense at all. Kimmie frowned, suddenly not sure she could believe her ex. People didn't make someone their emergency contact after a one-night stand.

"Tina was shot in a drive-by shooting."

"Oh no." Kimmie walked faster, reaching the water. As a journalist, she felt the shock of the accident. They all accepted the risks of their jobs. But when one of them got hurt, everyone shared their pain. "Travis, I don't know what to say."

"It was bad."

"Tell me about it." Kimmie folded up the legs of her baggy overalls and stepped into the water, letting the clear waves wash away the heat of the beach. It was hard for Travis to talk about this, but at least he did talk.

"She was in Miami, reporting on families of gang members, and just happened to be in the wrong place at the wrong time. She was alive, but that was about it. They patched her up as best they could, but she needed me to care for her."

"She did?"

"That's what the hospital told me. By the time they called, she was in surgery and it wasn't clear whether she'd come out again. I didn't ask questions. I just went."

Kimmie shook her head, utterly confused. "Okay."

"She survived, but the bullet had nicked her spine. She wanted me to bring her back to England. I did bring her back. And I stayed to take care of her."

"Oh." It was like being caught in a whirlpool. Whenever Kimmie thought she had a grasp on what had happened, Travis said something else that whisked the rug out from under her. She focused on the water sloshing over her feet to stay in the moment.

"Are you okay, Kimmie?"

"I don't know. I had no idea all that was going on, Travis. I thought you got fed up with me working too much. Or worst-case scenario, you had an affair. I guess...I'm really sorry for Tina. But I don't understand why it had to be you."

He exhaled. "Hang on. I'll be back in a mo." He went away and she heard him talking, but not the words.

Then he was back. "I couldn't face seeing you again. I knew I wasn't able to deal with you on top of everything else that was happening. I was drowning, Kimmie."

"I'm sorry, Travis." Kimmie frowned, and then she took a selfish plunge. "Only I *still* don't understand why it has to be you. I mean, you were my *husband*. Didn't she have family or friends?" Why did he have to take care of a woman he'd only met briefly, who hadn't wanted a relationship with him? What was he not telling her?

"It had to be me, Kimmie," he said. "She needs me more than you. You were always independent. You never needed me."

"How is she now?" Kimmie asked after a moment. Love or no love, married or not—it felt cruel to compete with someone in Tina's situation. Maybe Travis was right; she didn't need him. And yet it felt all sorts of wrong to lose him to another woman.

"It's tough. Some of the wounds never healed properly. She's still in and out of the hospital with infections and other complications. There's a lot going on, but...it's too much to talk about."

Kimmie's toes were suddenly freezing. She stepped into the dry sand and sat, feeling drained. Travis made it clear that the photographer still needed him. "I'm sorry about that, Travis. I hope she'll be okay."

"I hope so too." The short syllables conveyed sadness and exhaustion.

"What are you going to do?" she whispered.

"Take it day by day. Right now she's in the hospital for observation. It's tough."

"Do you want to come here while she's in the hospital? Not for me. To get yourself back together—even if it's just for a few days. You can have my house, and I'll stay with my mom."

He made a strange sound. "I don't think that's a good idea."

"I understand." It was an eight-hour flight. And maybe he thought she was trying to trick him into abandoning the woman he clearly loved. But much as Kimmie missed him, Travis had chosen his path.

"I wish her all the best," she said. "Let me know if I can do anything to help. I don't want anything in return, Travis." She turned her face into the sun, trying to get warm again. "I miss you, and I'm glad we finally talked, Trav. But you're right. I don't need you. Not the way Tina does."

When he spoke, his voice was muffled as if he'd shifted the phone away from his mouth. "How are you, Kimmie?"

He hadn't asked her before—another wall down, another defense dropped. Kimmie's lip twitched into a small smile. All she could do for him—and herself—was to forgive.

"I'm sitting pretty in Maine," Kimmie said, trying to sound cheerful. "My new house is more or less on the beach. I met someone I like a lot." It was true. She did like Bennett a lot. It didn't matter that Bennett would never be more than a friend. But if Travis thought she'd moved on, he could let go of feeling guilty.

"That sounds nice. I'm glad." He exhaled. "I'm so glad, Kimmie."

"Maybe we'll see each other again sometime," Kimmie said because she couldn't keep the words back. "Maybe when Tina is better, you can both visit. Everyone seems to be getting better here. There's something in the air."

"If we can, we will." He sounded doubtful.

"It's called Bay Harbor," Kimmie reminded him. "In Maine. Write it down and tuck it away. And then come visit sometime. I'll still have the house here."

He didn't respond for so long she thought he'd ended the call. "Travis?" she asked. "Do you have to go?"

"I'd better. Bye, Kimmie. I'm glad you called."

"Me too. Bye, Travis."

"Hey. For what it's worth...I'm sorry."

"Yeah. I'm sorry too." Kimmie let her phone sink.

At least now she knew it was over.

CHAPTER 26

Lovie's eyes closed, and she turned her head until her cheek—still rosy from nursing—rested on the cool mattress. The rosebud lips opened, and the tight little fists stilled as if she'd fallen asleep in the middle of a protest.

Sisley sat beside the crib until her baby's chest rose and fell to the rhythm of her dreams.

Then she rose and adjusted the curtains to dim the bright light of the late morning. She folded a couple of laundered onesies and straightened the teddy bear and the woolly lamb. After that was done, she could find no more reason to stay, so she picked up the baby monitor and softly stepped out of the nursery, shutting the door behind her.

Her hand on the handle, she listened to the sounds of the house. There was the rushing of the sea and the on-and-off hum of the honey extractor but no more voices murmuring on the patio.

Sisley went into the bathroom, washed her hands and face, and slipped out of her pj's and into one of Grandma Julie's 70s dresses with massive flower-girl vibes. She brushed her hair and put on sunscreen, and then she lost the challenge she'd set herself and peeked out of the window after all. It was the only one from which the entire patio was visible.

Bennett was gone.

Sisley exhaled. Good. Good, good, good.

She looked again, just to make sure.

He was still gone, but now she spotted Kimmie across the field, returning from a beach walk. The wind was tousling her sister's short hair which was as black as Sisley's was blond. Something in Kimmie's step, the bend of her neck, or the slope of her shoulders, made Sisley frown. Kimmie stopped and pulled out her phone.

Sisley's own phone beeped. She fetched it from the side of the sink and checked the screen.

Kimmie. She was going to go to her house, and to let Mom know she wasn't going to be there for lunch.

Sisley texted back she would tell Mom, and then she watched as Kimmie changed her course, cutting to the street.

Sisley wanted to call her, ask if she was okay. But then she remembered Bennett and the way Kimmie had looked at him and decided that despite saying she didn't mind, maybe Kimmie didn't want to talk with her right now.

She sighed because Bennett was everything she'd ever wanted in a man. It was exactly how she'd felt about Lars in the beginning.

Sisley went into her room. She'd never filled in her goldfinch drawing with watercolors like she'd meant to do. Now Mom or maybe Sunny had hung it—upside down again—on the wall in the entrance.

She picked up the case of watercolors and put it in an old straw tote. Like the dress, it had been her grandmother's. Then she added some brushes, a small jar with tap water, and a sketchbook with paper that was thick enough for aquarelles.

She couldn't go all the way to the beach because the baby monitor didn't reach that far. But she could go halfway down the field and stand in the middle of wildflowers and waving grass and paint the colors, the movements, the lines of water and sky and dunes.

Sisley slung the straw bag over her shoulder and hitched up her skirt to see the stairs, and then she made her way downstairs, out the patio, and into the field.

When the baby monitor started to buzz with static, she backtracked until she could hear her daughter breathe again, and then she left the trodden path and went sideways into the flowers and the grass until she felt like stopping and sitting down. The stalks and blades grew so high their tips swayed over her head, covering her view of the sea, and the house, and anything but the sky.

She pulled out the sketchbook and found a spot for her water jar and the paints. She sat, legs crossed and book on her knees, and started painting. She didn't use a method, at least none taught at college, but simply let the brush go here and there, however it felt good. Not all of the strokes looked the way she wanted them to look, but she didn't stop, and she didn't mind.

Instead, she let herself sink into the picture forming under her brush strokes. The ochers of burned sand and ripe seeds faded to the blues of summer sky and water.

The wind rose and tousled the grass like a hand caressing it. *"Beautiful."*

Sisley almost dropped her brush; the voice had been so unexpected. She couldn't jump up because of the wet paper on her knees, but she craned her neck. "Hello?"

There was only silence. Even the wind that stirred the grass had moved on.

Sisley's heart was beating hard, and instinctively, her hand went to pick up the baby monitor and press it to her ear. In the house, her baby was sleeping calmly, snuffling now and then. There was no one else in the room.

She set it down again. The paint had dried on the paper into a riot of color that showed no shape or form. But to her, it made sense. When she looked at it, she could smell seed-heavy stalks, feel grainy sand under her feet, and salty seawater drying on warm skin.

Sisley closed the sketchbook.

Maybe she was going crazy... First, a voice that sounded like someone standing behind her and looking over her shoulder. Then she was sensing a painting.

She shook her head to shift her brain back into place.

Maybe the voice had come from the baby monitor after all. Maybe she'd been too absorbed to notice.

She emptied her jar into the thirsty ground and stuffed her painting supplies back into the straw bag, hitched up Grandma Julie's dress, and stood. She cast a glance around. No. There was nobody else in the field.

Sisley hurried back to the house, taking the steps to the nursery two at a time. When she reached the top, she stopped.

The door was closed.

She could *feel* there was nobody in there.

There was nobody in Lovie's room, whispering over the sleeping baby.

She carefully opened the door, then tiptoed to the crib.

Lovie was still on her back, raising her legs and dropping them on the mattress, sucking on a fist, and staring at Sisley with big eyes.

Sisley had to laugh. "Aww, sweetheart, are you awake?"

She picked up her baby and sniffed, wrinkling her nose. "You need a change." She kissed the warm forehead, and Lovie gurgled and waved her wet hands at Sisley's cheeks, which made Sisley laugh more. Then she set to work changing Lovie's diaper. When the baby was clean, Sisley picked up a soft white shirt with tiny stitched flowers.

Small as it was, it had way too many buttons, all of them hard to snap shut. She was still fiddling with them when someone knocked on the door. "Mom," she called, exasperated. "Come do the rest of the buttons, or Lovie is going to go naked."

"It's just me. But I'm rather good with buttons."

Sisley swiveled on her heel. Bennett stood in the open door. He lifted a straw hat he was holding.

"Your mom asked me to get this for her," he explained. "I didn't mean to scare you, but I heard someone in here and I thought I'd seen you in the field, so... Once a cop, always a cop, I'm afraid." The skin by his eyes crinkled. "You look... Did I scare you? I'm sorry."

"I'm all right." Sisley felt a warm blush crawl up her neck. "I thought you were Mom." She turned away. The way he looked at her felt too much like Lars had looked at her a long time ago. She left the last buttons open and picked up the baby, a shield between her and Bennett.

She walked toward the door without meeting his eyes. Bennett stepped aside to make space, and Sisley continued to the stairs and started to descend.

He followed her. "I did scare you, didn't I?" It wasn't a question but a statement.

She stopped at the bottom of the stairs. Mom and Sunny, Peter and Amelie, and Charlie were sitting outside, hot from working in the honey barn, drinking iced tea, laughing.

Relieved they weren't alone, Sisley finally looked up at Bennett. He had only meant to make sure Lovie was safe, and suddenly, she realized how ungracious and silly she behaved. She owed him more than that.

"I was out in the field painting, and I heard a voice. But there was nobody there, so I thought someone was in the room with Lovie. *That* scared me." She smiled an apology. "I'm just short on sleep. Thank you for checking on her."

"You heard a voice on the baby monitor?" He frowned. "How fast did you get to the room?"

"Oh!"

She turned. Mom was standing at the open door, staring at her. "Mom?"

"Oh my goodness." Mom put a hand to her heart, and her lips twitched. "For a second, I thought I saw my mother." She squeezed her eyes shut. "You almost gave me a heart attack."

Sisley went to her mother and hugged her. Mom had told her tons of times that she looked like Julie. "It's the dress," she said and laughed as she stepped back to do a swirl.

"You have her figure and the hair, even her *shoulders*." Mom shook her head. "Standing there with your back to me, you looked exactly like I remember her."

"I scared you," Sisley repeated the words Bennett had said to her.

"I've been in the heat too long." Mom reached for Lovie, who was kicking her little legs like a frog, and Sisley handed her over. "Come on out, darlings." Mom turned. "I have peach milkshakes for you and Bennett."

Bennett handed Sisley Mom's hat. "I'll just have a quick look around Lovie's nursery if that's okay. Just...routine."

"I really think I was daydreaming. But go ahead. I like knowing she's safe."

He nodded and turned. The steps groaned under his feet, and then she heard him creak over the old floorboards into Lovie's room. As best she could tell, he went from window to window.

She wondered if he would check the other bedrooms, but he seemed to go to the bathroom. Something thumped, and his footsteps quieted.

Mom reappeared. She'd already lost Lovie to someone else. Sisley glanced out the door and saw Peter rocking the baby.

"Why aren't you coming out?" Mom asked. "Where did Bennett get to?"

"I think he's checking the attic for invaders," Sisley said. "I heard a voice in the nursery earlier, but I was just daydreaming."

Mom looked at her. "What attic?"

Sisley grinned. "Didn't you see the trapdoor in the bathroom ceiling?"

"The bathroom ceiling? I don't think I ever looked at the bathroom ceiling."

"There's a wooden stick with a hook in the towel cabinet to pull it open."

"Is that what that is?"

Sisley raised an eyebrow. "What did you think it was for, Mom? Catching fish in the bathtub?"

"I thought it was an olden-time laundry thing. You know, to pull the line in or something."

Sisley couldn't help but laugh. "Really, Mom, you've been too rich for too long."

"Well, how do *you* know about attic sticks?"

"I had one in my college apartment," Sisley said. Just the thought of the apartment she'd share with Lars made her somber. She crossed her arms.

There was another thud upstairs, and a minute later, Bennett appeared on the stairs. "No one upstairs as far as I can tell," he announced and fished a cobweb from his hair. "Though I didn't want to go in the bedrooms."

"You found an attic, I hear." Mom peeked around Sisley.

Bennett stepped on the landing and brushed dust off his shoulder. "You have a lot of stuff up there," he remarked. "It's none of my business, but it could be a fire hazard. With a baby in the house, it might be worth cleaning that out."

"I will, now that I know there is one!" Mom said. "But for the moment, let's go outside and drink the milkshakes while they're cold."

CHAPTER 27

When Sisley came outside, Peter stood up. "Do you want Lovie back?" he asked guiltily.

She smiled. "Keep her if you like. I don't mind."

"She's the sweetest little pea." He sat back down and tickled Lovie's foot.

"Sit with me." Her great-aunt patted the chair beside her.

"How are you doing, Sunny?" Sisley asked and took the offered seat. Mom handed her a glass of peach shake and sat beside Peter.

"Waiting for the surgery," Sunny said miserably. "They got me in extra early."

"So it's over soon." Sisley took Sunny's hand. "Right?"

"Next week." The words came out as a whisper. Sunny cleared her voice and tried again. "Next week, and I'm scared to death. But I'm going to do it anyway."

"That's the spirit. You got this." Sisley knew something about being scared. She vividly remembered seeing the small blue line on the pregnancy test. She'd been scared to tell Lars.

She turned, trying to get away from the memory, and met Bennett's watchful eyes.

She turned back again. "What happens after the surgery?" she asked. "Can you come back right away?"

"If it goes well, yes, I can come home fairly quickly. If not...we'll see."

Sisley patted her aunt's hand. "It'll go well. I can feel it."

"You can feel it?" Sunny smiled wistfully. "That's what your grandma used to say. I can feel this, I can feel that. I used to tease her for it."

"And?" Julie was popping up a lot today. "Was she right?"

Sunny sighed as if she'd lost a bet. "You know what? Often enough. I didn't really keep track, but I remember saying she would have to eat her words. It was always me who ended up wrong."

"Sis? Where's Kimmie? Do you know?" Mom interrupted them. "I thought she was here. And Jo? Where'd she get to?"

"Oh. I was supposed to tell you Kimmie's gone to her house," Sisley reported. "I don't know about Johanna. She was here for breakfast, but she was gone when I came back."

"She's supposed to move into Kimmie's room," Mom said. "Did she bring any luggage with her?"

"I don't know. I came down late for breakfast, and I didn't ask her about it."

"That's okay. I'll call her later." Mom frowned the frown she only had when she was worried about one of her kids and exchanged a quick look with Peter.

"So Johanna's moving in then?" She didn't know Jo as well as Kimmie did; only that she'd been gone and why.

"I hope so. She's going to help Sunny with her recovery while she starts her online business as a PA." Mom looked worried as if she wasn't sure Johanna would come through.

"I'll go see Kimmie," Sisley decided on the spur of the moment. "I haven't had a tour of the new house yet. And I'll let you know if I see Johanna." She emptied her glass and stood.

"I don't want you to do too much," Mom got up as well. She took Lovie from Peter, who was distracted talking with Charlie, and walked Sisley into the house. "You're still recovering, sweetheart. Your body needs time to heal."

Sisley kissed her cheek. How had she not noticed Lars didn't love her? How had she forgotten the way it was when someone cared? "I feel fine. I got lucky." She smiled. "And I promise to take a break when I need one."

"Remember you do. Things need time to snap back into place." Mom patted her arm. "Now shoo. Go see your sister. Don't lift anything and have her drive you back. If Lovie gets hungry, I'll come get you."

Lovie was blowing spit bubbles. Sisley stroked the soft hair. "Thanks, Mom."

She left to walk down the empty street. The walk wasn't likely to do much harm, for sure. There were only two houses between Mom and Kimmie. They looked empty but not neglected. Maybe they were someone's vacation homes?

A building boom in nearby towns, followed by a downturn in the economy, had left many Bay Harbor houses empty. But there was also a sprinkle of second or vacation homes. Sisley found herself wondering whether the two houses between Mom and Kimmie were for sale.

But there was no point in finding out—even with help, there was no way she could afford one. Knowing it was available would only make her want it that much more. And Sisley was grateful for all she had received since coming to Bay Harbor. She wanted to stay grateful.

Sisley walked past a gorgeous oceanfront cottage, swallowing a feeling of longing. What a house to call one's own... It would have a garden and a view similar to Mom's, and even though there'd be some rocks to climb over, the house would have its own beach access.

She bowed her head, hurrying past to Kimmie's house. It was painted the soft green of the first spring leaves. All Sisley knew about it was that it had three bedrooms and a guest room. What she didn't know was what Kimmie would do with all that space.

Mature hydrangeas and rhododendrons fringed the path and blocked the view from the street into the backyard; blue and pink clouds of petals waved in the sea breeze, perfuming the air with a sweet scent that reminded Sisley of jasmine.

Sisley pressed her lips together as she went up the short path to the door, again squelching any burgeoning feelings of wanting her own house. She rang the doorbell and stepped back to wait.

A full minute later, the door opened, and Kimmie's face appeared. "Oh," she said. "I thought it was the mailman."

Sisley gave her a look and, without asking, squished past her sister into the house. "You're crying." She put down the linen bag that served as her purse.

"I *was* crying," Kimmie corrected her and closed the door.

"Why? What happened?"

Kimmie waved her to follow. The house had an open floorplan and living room, dining room, and kitchen combined into a single large space. "I know," Kimmie gestured at the walls as she sat on the sofa. "It needs work."

"I didn't say that," Sisley said. "But if you want my opinion, I think it's adorable." There was a fireplace large enough to warm the house even in the depth of winter, enough glass to bathe the room in sunlight, and a Scandinavian theme of polished, hazelnut-colored wood and white brick. "It is so cozy. Very different from your New York City apartment." Sisley walked around, touching this and that, trying again not to imagine herself and Lovie in a house like this. "All you need are some big plants and chunky blankets. Maybe some braided poofs and fake sheepskin rugs. You could put some of your travel photographs on the walls. And obviously, those cute built-in bookshelves need books."

"Hmm." Kimmie seemed to have lost her earlier enthusiasm for the new home.

"Can I sit?"

"You don't have to ask, Sis." Kimmie frowned. "Why are you here? You're not supposed to walk far."

"I hardly walked far, coming from Mom's house. I'm fine." But when Sisley sat next to her sister, she did notice a twinge or two. Even an easy birth was taxing on the body. She leaned back to get comfortable, grateful this sofa was more soft than modern. "Oof. All right. Can I say something?"

"Stop asking for permission. It's weird." Kimmie rubbed her face and ran her fingers through her hair. "What's up?"

"I was serious when I said I'm not looking," Sisley said quickly.

Kimmie shook her head. "I have no idea what you are talking about. Looking for what?"

"A relationship. I know we talked about it already, but—"

"Oh." Kimmie leaned back and crossed her arms. She looked tired. Her eyelids were red. "This again?"

Sisley tilted her head. "You like Bennett. I know you do."

Kimmie shrugged. "Sure I do. Who wouldn't? He's a great guy."

"So?"

"So nothing. That's all. I'm not looking either."

Sisley fell back into the plush sofa. "I thought you were interested?"

"Of course not."

"Okay," Sisley said slowly. "My mistake. Sorry. It's just, you looked miserable walking back from the beach earlier. I thought it was because...never mind. Obviously not."

"I didn't see you." Kimmie studied her fingernails. They were short and clean and there was no reason to look at them. "It had nothing to do with Bennett."

"No?"

"I talked with Travis."

"Travis?" Sisley felt her eyes widen. As far as she knew, Travis divorced her sister without a word, and there'd been no peep from the man since. "Did he call you?"

"Sort of. He called but hung up, and I had a feeling it was him. So today I called back. He said it was an accident that he called me, but I'm not sure."

"Wow. What did he say?"

Kimmie took a breath, and then she told Sisley.

CHAPTER 28

Mela put the leftover gazpacho into the fridge, closed the door, and glanced at her phone.

She'd gotten a text from each Sisley and Kimmie earlier, both saying they would have lunch at Kimmie's place. Johanna wasn't with them.

After a brief struggle, Mela dialed Johanna's phone again, promising herself it was the last time. But unlike before, now there was a response. "Johanna!" She tried not to squeak with relief. "Where are you? What happened?"

"Hi, Mela. Nothing happened. I just felt restless and wanted to drive down the coast a bit to clear my head. I'm in a small town called Beach Cove. It's lovely, but the phone reception is pretty bad. Did you call before? Do you need something?"

Mela exhaled. "I don't need anything; I was worried about you. I thought you would move in today, but I don't see any of your things anywhere. Are we still doing this?"

"I'm sorry." Johanna's faint voice cut in and out. "I don't have very much, and it's all in my car. Kimmie's things were still in the room upstairs, and it didn't feel right to hurry her out."

"Oh, she's already got her things in the new house, Johanna. Whatever is in that room is old stuff—we'll pack it up and stow it away. I just learned I have a whole walkable attic under the roof. We can put the boxes there until I can get a donation truck to pick them up."

"Okay."

"So...when will you be back?" Like a mother hen, Mela wanted the young woman close. Not sitting lonely in some parking lot, staring out at the sea.

"Soon," Johanna said. Suddenly, her voice was crystal clear. "I'm having lunch at a diner in the harbor. Breaded flounder. It's delicious."

"Well, do you think you'll be back for dinner tonight? Amelie and I were thinking about making lasagna together."

"I'm not sure; I might stay the night. I met a nice lady who used to be a fishmonger, but now she's running an inn with her best friend. They're usually booked out but had a cancellation." Johanna chuckled. "She said I looked like I needed a good night's rest and could stay for free. She also said to go swimming and then see whether I feel like taking her up on her offer or driving back to Bay Harbor."

"Okay. Well, let me know when you decide. Either way, see you soon, my dear. Enjoy yourself." Kimmie had already told Mela about Beach Cove. If Jo enjoyed Bay Harbor, it made sense she would fall in love with the white beaches of Beach Cove as well.

"I will," Johanna said. "Thank you for checking on me." For the first time in a long time, Mela heard a smile in her voice.

"I just wanted to say, Jo—I'm looking forward to having you in the house. You are not alone. I'm here. We're in this with you."

"Okay," Johanna replied. "Thank you."

"Call me." Mela waited until Johanna ended the call.

Peter came into the kitchen, carrying Lovie. "I think she wants her mama. She's getting cranky."

"Aww." Mela kissed first the baby's head, then Peter, and then she texted Sisley.

Be right there, Sisley texted back immediately. *Kimmie will drive me.*

"The girls are coming back together." Mela let her phone sink, feeling her heart lift. "They've spent more time in each other's company last week than in the last ten years."

"That's good." Peter nodded his approval.

The sliding door to the patio opened, and Charlie came in. "Amelie wandered off to pick flowers. She told me to tell you."

Mela smiled. She liked to know where everyone was. "Thank you, Charlie. The grass is so high it becomes hard to see who left and who's still around, picking flowers in the field."

"Should we go back outside?" Charlie raised a questioning eyebrow. He was almost as handsome as Peter. "I feel cold when I'm not in the sun."

Peter chuckled. "It's hardly cold. The forecast was for a high of eighty-six."

"Actually, I meant to go and check on the bees," Mela said. "But I have a few more minutes. Let's have a cup of coffee, no?"

The men agreed, and Mela brewed a strong pot. Sisley and Kimmie arrived, and while Kimmie plopped down in the living room to check her email on her phone, Sisley went upstairs to nurse and catch a nap with Lovie. When the coffee was ready, Mela brought Kimmie a cup, then filled three more mugs and carried them outside.

"You're still staying in Sandville, aren't you?" Mela sat beside Charlie. Charlie hadn't taken Peter up on the invitation to stay in Bay Harbor.

Charlie nodded and crossed his legs. "I was going to ask about the motel, Peter."

Peter looked up. He'd been watching the steam curling from his mug. "I told you everything there's to know, Charlie. Don't worry about staying in Sandville—I get it. No need to dig up bad memories."

Mela knew that his brother's story had deeply shaken Peter. He had a tough time sleeping, his mind busy putting together bits and pieces that finally made sense.

"I don't feel guilty about staying in Sandville." Charlie grinned his charming cowboy smile. "I was going to make a business proposition."

Judging from Peter's motionless face, he was as surprised as Mela.

What business proposition could Charlie possibly make? As far as Mela understood, he had a ranch in Australia. He and Peter didn't even live on the same continent.

"Go ahead," Peter encouraged him. "What did you have in mind?"

"When I came back, I didn't come because of Amelie. Or, to be perfectly honest, you." Charlie folded his hands. "Much as I wanted to see the two of you, I had no idea you lived in Bay Harbor."

"So why did you come back?" Mela asked, curious. To her, it seemed pretty obvious that Charlie *had* been searching for Amelie. And to her surprise, Amelie wasn't mad about it. On the contrary, her friend seemed happier than ever before.

"I changed my mind on a few things in the last few years. It came on gradually." He stopped abruptly as if there was a whole lot more but no time to say it. "It boils down to this: I was homesick. After all these years, I needed to see the coast of Maine. So I came." He looked at Peter. "I'd have come earlier had I known all of you were here. And if I'd known I've got a grown son—" He stopped.

Mela put her hand on his arm. "You're here now. And you finally found your family."

"I'm still in shock. I feel lucky Bennett is even talking to me."

"Life is complicated, and Bennett is smart enough to know it."

"What was the business proposition you had in mind?" Peter asked.

Charlie picked up a napkin, turning it between his fingers. "I would like to offer to buy half the motel."

Peter leaned into his chair. "What do you mean?"

"I want to buy my way into your business. We'd be partners, running the motel together. We share costs and profits. If you like."

"There are plenty of costs; you've seen the motel. It's a money pit. There are very few tourists in Bay Harbor." Peter cleared his throat. "Let me correct myself. There are no tourists at all in Bay Harbor. You're the only traveler who's stopped by in the last...oh, I don't know. It's been years."

"Are you in touch with the people that used to rent a room or two?"

"Dad saw to it those contacts turned sour. I figure those who still travel found new places to go to," Peter responded.

Charlie looked out at the sea. "Can't say I'm surprised. But this is not about making money. I'm doing well enough without the motel." He stood and walked to the wall. "I want to reclaim my past. I want to change how I remember this place. Already...look at all that happened already. I came thinking I'd hate everything but the sea and found Am—Um." He swallowed his mistake. "I found a son. It means a lot to me."

He wants to mend a wound, Mela thought. She, too, had returned with a lot of painful memories. The sea had taken her mother and uncle. But the small town had called her back to embrace her, reunite her with old friends, and give her love and family. Her life was so different now, and she was much happier. "I understand exactly what you mean, Charlie," she said.

Peter spread his hands. "I don't mind sharing the old place with you."

"Let's talk numbers later," Charlie said. "I want in on financing the renovation. Once we have her fixed up, we'll set about getting all those rooms filled."

Peter crossed his arms. "What sort of ranch are you running over in Australia?" he asked. "Big, small, medium?"

Charlie leaned back as well, mirroring his older brother. "Biggish."

Mela stood. "I'm going for a quick look at the bees. You stay and talk—there's cheesecake in the fridge and fresh raspberries to go with it if you want something sweet."

The brothers got up, and Peter kissed Mela. "Take care of yourself," he murmured. "I don't like you going out there by yourself."

She smiled. "Why? I'm only going to a field full of flowers."

He cradled her cheek in his hand. "I'm worried the bees are going to get you."

"Not allergic, remember? I do not react to bee stings."

"Call me every ten minutes."

She chuckled. "No, I won't. But I'll be back to have a slice of cake before dinner." Mela rose on her tiptoes and pressed another kiss on his cheek, and then she left. She wasn't worried about doing bee work alone. What was the worst that could happen?

CHAPTER 29

Mela parked her car in the shade of an oak on the bluff. She was wearing three-quarter pants and a brightly colored shirt. The fabric wasn't very thick and didn't cover all of her, but it would do.

She took her water and hive tool from the backseat of the car and walked through the tall grass toward the bees. The warm air hummed with the buzz of crickets and cicadas. To Mela, it was a happy sound that took her right back to the summer afternoons she'd spent with her mother in their garden.

She wished Julie could see her hives now; she'd be so proud. They'd painted the old boxes in whites and yellows and blues; each hive had its distinct pattern on the front. It made it easier for foragers to find their homes when they returned from foraging trips.

A bee zipped past her as she got closer, then another. More and more followed until finally, Mela had to stop walking because a cloud of swirling, dancing bees trapped her.

She held her breath; she was not prepared to catch a swarm. Swarming bees didn't sting. But she still couldn't very well shove a glob of bees in the trunk of her car for safekeeping—or even back in the hive. The colony probably had a new queen already, and she'd fight the old one to the death.

Mela stood still, watching the bees dance in the afternoon light. There was no sense of direction here though a swarm always followed its queen. But these bees simply streamed out of the hives and flew ever-expanding circles around their entrances. Some even dropped back on the landing boards, scrambling against their exiting sisters, and disappeared into the darkness of the hive.

Mela leaned closer. Swarming bees wouldn't do that.

The bees weren't swarming. These were not seasoned foragers, ready to start over.

These were baby foragers, bees that so far had only done hive duties. Most of them had never been outside before. To them, everything was new. The grass, the sky, the scents... It was a lot to take in. "Good girls," Mela whispered. "Well done."

Instead of risking getting lost, these youngsters bravely launched themselves into the unknown—only to turn around for a good, long look at their hive. After all, if they were to bring back nectar and pollen, it was important to know how their home looked.

Mela waited. Orientation flights never took long. Satisfied and full of new impressions, the budding foragers soon crawled back into their hive.

When the bees were gone, Mela set to work opening the lids with her hive tool. She'd only just added the treatment for the deadly Varroa mites, but already, the covers were glued back to the topmost box of the hive by the workers.

She hadn't brought a smoker to distract the bees, and they launched themselves like tiny missiles at her. She stood still, letting them settle on her shoulders and arms, where they suspiciously rubbed their front legs together.

Carefully, Mela lifted out a frame, held her breath, and leaned in for a closer look.

There were no mites. "It's too early," she whispered and swapped the frame for another. Again, there wasn't a single mite.

Mela closed the hive and opened another, then one more, and the result was the same every time: there were no mites.

She sealed the boxes and wiped her hands on the grass. It couldn't have been her treatment, could it? It was too soon. Maybe, if the colonies had never been treated before, the mites had low resistance to the treatment?

Mela lay in between the wildflowers, picked a blade of sweetgrass, and chewed on it while blinking into the sky. Varroa could easily swipe out entire bee yards. Mela had gotten lucky—definitely more than she could explain. The heat, the humming, and the gentle swaying of the grass stalks made her sleepy.

She was just about to nod off when her phone vibrated in her pocket. Mela pulled it out and squinted at the screen. It was a number she didn't recognize, but the area code was local. She sat up. "Yes? This is Pamela Beckett."

"Hello, this is Valerie. I'm the chair of the Bay Harbor Farmers' Market. I just read your email and wanted to get back to you."

"Thank you for calling." Mela stood. "I was hoping to sell my honey at the market."

"That would be great," Valerie said. "The thing is, we are pretty full. There's a lot of competition for open spots. I don't want to use the word cutthroat, but, well..." She cleared her throat. "Of course we are always looking to improve the customer experience."

"So...uh, what does that mean?" Mela crossed her fingers that the news was better than this let on. "How do I apply for a stand?"

"Well, before we even start, let me ask you this: are you in compliance with all the necessary rules and regulations for selling honey?"

"I have an apiary license. Is that enough?"

There was a small sound that could have been either a laugh or a sigh. "You'll have to look into food safety licenses."

"Oh. Right." She bit her lip; she should've known it wouldn't be as easy as putting jars on a table. Now she felt stupid.

"Once you have everything together and are ready to *go*," Valerie continued, "get back in touch. And just a tip from someone who has been there—I know it's a small town, but this market is all about excellence. It's up to you of course, but if you can make your branding stand out, it helps to attract customers and keep your stand. Also, you might start thinking about a business strategy while you are at it."

"It would be more for fun," Mela said slowly.

"Fun?" Valerie repeated the word incredulously.

Mela brushed the dry grass off her legs. "Thank you for calling back and letting me know about all this, Valerie." Around her, the field was an oasis of peace that didn't fit words like branding and strategy. "I will look into everything you mentioned."

"You're *welcome*. Let me know when you're ready. Have a wonderful day now."

"You too." Mela ended the call.

A small breeze rose from the sea, playfully tugging on the grass.

She had decades of experience in marketing and branding. Easy enough to get that license—a call to arrange for an inspector to visit her honey barn, a red—no, yellow—ribbon and handwritten note tied to a cute jar she'd find online. A couple of cost-benefit spreadsheets, a pricing strategy; she'd have to look at what competitors did and...and...

The breeze blew again, warm and soft, and suddenly, Mela relaxed and let go.

Maybe later.

Right now, she had enough on her hands. Sunny's surgery, Baby Lovie, Kimmie's new house, Johanna, the motel... She wanted to spend her time with family and friends, not making spreadsheets and searching the internet and setting up appointments. It was so easy to get too busy.

It had been Julie's dream to sell her honey at the farmers' market. But she had been young and looking for an income doing what she loved. Mela had only a bucket list.

"Sorry, Mom. I'll get around to it eventually," Mela whispered. As if in response, the breeze brushed her hair aside and kissed her forehead.

Sisley looked so much like her grandmother. It was uncanny.

Mela stood for a while longer, thinking of daughters and mothers and the wind, and then she picked up her hive tool and drove back home.

CHAPTER 30

Sisley hugged Sunny. Her great-aunt felt tense and tight, standing like a tin soldier in the driveway, hospital bag at the ready. "It'll be worth it," Sisley whispered in her ear. "You'll see."

"Cross your fingers," Sunny said, her voice higher than usual. She cleared her throat. "If you don't mind. Just in case."

"All fingers crossed." Sisley kissed Sunny's cheek and let go so Kimmie could take her place.

"Think of the beach walks you'll take," Kimmie said and kissed her great-aunt's other cheek. "It'll all be worth it." She let go and scooted over to make space for Johanna.

"Don't fuss, all right? Just get in and out." She gave Sunny a quick hug and turned away.

"Will do, honey," Sunny said to her back.

Sisley went to Johanna and put an arm around her. Letting her beloved Sunny go into surgery, however routine, was difficult for Jo right now. She'd even considered not coming back after all because of it, but a couple of days thinking it over in Beach Cove had changed her mind.

"Everything's going to be fine," Sisley said firmly.

"Are you all done saying bye?" Mela called out from the car. "We kind of have to go!" She was already sitting in the driver's seat, triple checking a bunch of papers.

"Yep! Here she comes!" Kimmie took Sunny's arm and helped her in the car.

Sisley let go of Johanna and went to peek around the propped-up hood of the car. Peter stood there, staring at the car's oil dipstick.

Gently, Sisley took the dipstick from Peter's hands. "She'll be all right," she repeated. "The car has plenty of oil." She put the stick back where it belonged.

"I know. I wish she had lost more weight, though. What if..."

"She'll be all right. She'll be more than all right; she'll be able to get around on her own again," Sisley promised. "I know she will."

Peter sighed and ran a hand through his hair, but then he nodded and reached up to shut the hood. "Well then, all good to go." He pulled a rag from the back pocket of his jeans and wiped his hands.

"Peter, tell me the truth," Sunny said miserably. "Am I going to survive this? It's major surgery."

Sisley grabbed his hand.

His fingers clenched hers. "Yes," he said. "Of course, Sunny. I'll have cheese sandwiches ready when you come back. No Swiss."

Sunny muttered something and nodded resignedly. Sisley squeezed Peter's hand back. He was doing well.

Mela set the papers aside, checked her purse one last time, and started the car.

They all waved, the car rolled down Seasweet, and Sunny was gone.

"I really hope the doctor knows what he's doing," Johanna said.

"Of course he does," Kimmie said mechanically. "Don't jinx it."

"He should have had plenty of practice," Peter said and crossed his arms. "Right?"

Sisley smiled. "I'm going to leave you worrywarts to it," she announced. "Lovie is going to wake up any moment."

Kimmie turned. "Can I come and say hi? She's been asleep since I got here."

"Sure."

"I'll stay with you, Peter." Johanna went to stand by Peter, who patted her shoulder distractedly. "At least we can be worrywarts together."

He stopped and threw her a look. "Want to have a look at the truck? Something's making a strange noise."

"I don't know the first thing about engines. But yes, please."

"It would help if you could just tell me whether there *is* a noise or whether I'm crazy."

"Have fun, you two." Sisley waved her sister to come, and together, she and Kimmie went inside and up the stairs.

"Is she still asleep?" Kimmie whispered once they got in front of the nursery door.

Instead of a reply, Sisley pulled the baby monitor from her pocket and held it out. Humming noises came from it, interrupted by small wet sounds. "She's blowing spit bubbles. She's getting good, too."

Kimmie grinned. "Aww. So the little monster is awake." She pressed on the door handle and, without waiting for Sisley, made a beeline for the crib.

"Hiiii," she cooed. Sisley, who had made plenty of silly sounds for Lovie herself, had to swallow a laugh. It didn't quite work, and she had to clear her throat.

Kimmie didn't hear or didn't mind, scooping up the baby, who happily swatted at her face. "Are you a little octopus?" she murmured. "Yes, you are!" She crinkled her nose. "Oof, Sis, I think your baby needs a fresh diaper."

"Oh, I see." Sisley took Lovie to the changing table. "So now she's *my* baby."

"Yep. All yours." Kimmie came to watch, only turning away to avoid the view of the diaper.

Sisley giggled. "It's not that bad yet. I hear it gets worse when they start to eat solids."

"You'll cross that bridge when you get to it," Kimmie said encouragingly. She picked up an outfit. "I got her this. Put it on, okay? I haven't seen her in it yet."

"It's very cute." It really was cute. Light green fabric, printed with tiny ladybugs. Sisley didn't mention the long row of snap buttons that went from collar to toe.

"Here, she's all clean. *You* put it on, darling," she said in Mela's voice.

"Watch and learn, little sister." Kimmie started to pull the sleeves over the tiny arms while Sisley dropped into the nursing glider to watch.

Lovie had been awake most of the previous night, and so had she. She'd opened the window and rocked her daughter in the dark. There had been a night bird singing a rhythmic melody. When she looked it up on her phone the next morning, she found it was a whip-poor-will.

Kimmie shook her head impatiently. "Goodness, what's with these buttons? They're taking ages to snap shut. It's hard to line them up too. Ugh. I missed one and now...aww, I gotta undo all these, or there's a gap." Lovie wiggled her arms, and Kimmie tickled her until Lovie suddenly went quiet. "Uh, Sis? I think she needs a new diaper again. Is that...normal?"

Sisley propped her elbow onto the armrest and her chin into her hand. "Perfectly. Go ahead, auntie. You're doing great."

Resigned, Kimmie held up a pack of wipes. "These?"

"Yep."

"All right. Come here, octopus." Kimmie started to undo the buttons again.

Sisley watched for a while. Then she asked, "Have you heard anything more from Travis? It's been a week since you two talked."

Kimmie glanced at her. "No. Why would he call?"

"Just a feeling he might. It was a strange story."

"Wasn't it?" Kimmie discarded the diaper and fished a new one from the stack. "Strange or not, it's pretty clear he's picked his battle."

"I guess."

Kimmie looked up. "You *guess*? Why do you sound so undecided?"

"Don't listen to me when it comes to relationship stuff, obviously." Sisley started to gently rock again. "Those diapers are still too big," she said. "Take one of the tiny ones."

Kimmie put back the size one and picked up a newborn diaper. "I was thinking," she said casually and lifted Lovie to slide the diaper under her.

"About what?"

"About...I don't know. Life and all that."

"What exactly about it?" Sisley stopped rocking.

"My editor got in touch and asked if I was interested in taking on a human rights project."

"Human rights?" Human rights projects took Kimmie to places where human rights weren't upheld. Sisley lifted her feet off the ottoman. "Like where?"

"Like South America."

Sisley stood. "A project on the rights or a project on their violations?"

Kimmie picked up Lovie and snuggled her into the nook between her neck and chin. She avoided Sisley's eyes. "Human trafficking."

"Human *trafficking*? Kimmie, no. Please don't do it. Stay here with me and Lovie and Mom and... Just stay here with us." Sisley pressed her hands into a fist, desperately casting around for reasons her sister needed to stay. Kimmie had that look on her face... Sisley grabbed her new aquarelle and thrust it at Kimmie. "Here. This is a bribe. I'm begging you not to risk your life, Kimmie. Please say you'll stay."

Kimmie freed a hand and took the aquarelle without looking at it. "I already said yes, Sis," she said quietly. "I'm good at what I do. I have a shot at helping a lot of women and children."

Sisley felt tears rise in her throat. "Somebody else can do it," she whispered. "Let someone else go this time."

Kimmie rocked Lovie. "It'll be all right, Sis." She tried to smile.

The tears pushed upward until Sisley felt them spill on her cheeks. She wiped them away.

They'd just gotten close. She needed more time with her sister.

"Aw, Sisley, don't do that." Kimmie went to the baby swing and strapped Lovie in, then came to Sisley and hugged her. "Calm down, okay? Calm down. I want to talk to you."

Sisley did her best. "Just hormones," she managed to get out between sobs that sounded like hiccups. "I won't miss you or anything."

"Got it," Kimmie said. "Can you do me a favor while I'm gone?"

"No." Sisley took a long, hitching breath. "Like what?"

"Can you look after my house? Maybe even..." Kimmie pulled Sisley into the glider and sat on the ottoman, holding her hand. "Maybe even move in."

"Move into your *house*?" Sisley started to cry again because it was Kimmie's house, and she wanted Kimmie in it, eating chocolate croissants in her pj's instead of investigating human trafficking gangs.

"I thought you'd like to have more space. I could also ask Johanna if you want. Johanna would help with Lovie if you needed a hand. She's superefficient, just ask Mom. And she's scared of just about nothing. Which would be good since you're such a scaredy cat."

"You're the one scared of moon shadows." Sisley pulled her hand from Kimmie's to wipe her face with her sleeve.

"Well, if one of them turns out to be Slenderman, Johanna will kick his butt. She knows martial arts and I've seen her in action. The woman is small but wiry."

Sisley closed her eyes. "Is there anything I can say to make you stay, Kimmie?"

"It's my job, Sis," Kimmie said. "I'm starting to get a little itchy to work, and I was always going to only spend the summer here."

Sisley opened her eyes again. "It's because you talked with Travis," she said, having a sudden intuition. "You and Johanna both use stupid adrenaline-kick stuff to distract yourselves. You're sad he's gone and not coming back because it wasn't even about you, and now you can't fix it. All this time, you hoped you could fix it."

"Nope. No. It's my *job*. It's what I *do*."

Sisley pointed a finger at Kimmie. "It's a terrible trait to have. Go have therapy instead."

Kimmie sighed and stood. "Okay. Well, kiddo, I'm going. You want my house, you got it. You don't, maybe Johanna will water my spider plant."

Sisley stood too. "I'll water your stupid plant. I'll live in the house, and when you come back, I'll claim squatter rights. I'll do all sorts of damage to your...your..." She couldn't think of anything. "Your *walls*," she ended lamely and exhaled. "Oof."

"All right, tiger." Kimmie gently boxed Sisley's shoulder. "I'm glad we got that out there."

"When are you leaving?" Sisley asked and went to pick up her daughter. Unlike Kimmie, babies needed love and human contact.

"As soon as Sunny's back from surgery."

Only a few days, then? "Are you going to come downstairs?" Sisley looked back.

Her sister shook her head. "I have to make a call."

CHAPTER 31

The box slipped from Amelie's hands and smashed to the ground, spilling yarn and unraveling balls of wool everywhere. She straightened with a groan, pressing a hand into her lower back. The spare room was a complete mess, cluttered with abandoned craft projects, crates full of how-to books, and other homeless things. But with both Bennett and Meredith moving in, they'd need the extra space.

The doorbell chimed.

"Come in, Bennett!" she called out. "It's open!"

The door downstairs opened and fell back shut. "Amelie? Where are you?"

"Charlie?" She threw a glance in the mirror. She wasn't ready for visitors. "I'm upstairs. Just a moment." She hurried into the bathroom to wash the dust off her hands and face and run a brush through her frizzy curls. It didn't do much good. She frowned at her reflection.

She'd only seen Charlie twice in the last four days.

"Amelie?"

She hurried to the staircase. "I was cleaning. Hi, Charlie."

Charlie was smiling at her as she came down the stairs. "It reminds me of prom night, you standing there like that," she joked.

"I didn't pick you up. Remember?" He took her hand for a greeting and held it—longer than necessary.

They'd met at the school. He'd waited outside for her with a corsage of white roses. "I remember." Amelie pulled her hand back, gesturing at the living room instead. "Would you like to sit?"

"I'd like to. But I can't stay long."

"Oh?" Charlie had been spending most of his time with Peter, working out the logistics of their partnership and the motel renovations.

"I was hoping you would take a quick drive with me. Can you spare half an hour? I meant to ask earlier, but..." He shrugged an apology. "We were busy nailing down things at the motel. Quite literally."

Amelie rolled down the sleeves of her oversized button-down shirt. "Drive where?"

"For starters, we could go grab lunch. I'm starving. And I want to see a little more coast before I leave."

"You're leaving soon?" Amelie moistened her lips.

"Tonight, actually. I have to take care of a few things at the ranch."

"That's...so soon." She tried to smile. It had been clear he wasn't going to stay long. But she'd hoped for more time than this. She'd hoped Bennett and Charlie would get to know each other better.

"I'm glad you care." He opened the front door.

"Charlie, I can't go like this." Amelie gestured at her dirt-streaked shirt. Her yoga leggings were strictly for home use, too. "Give me ten minutes. Sit and take a breath. Get yourself something to drink—there's iced tea in the fridge."

He closed the door again. "Okay."

Amelie hurried upstairs and pulled out the white sheath dress she'd bought at the boutique last week. She slipped out of her cleaning clothes and into the crisp dress, rubbed some hair foam between her hands and scrunched her curls into shape, then did her best with mascara and lipstick. After a moment of hesitation—too much?—she puffed a squirt of perfume in the air and quickly walked through the cloud. Then she went downstairs.

Charlie was standing at the window, looking out at the yard. When he heard her, he turned. His throat moved when he saw her, but it took him a moment to speak. "You're beautiful, Amelie."

"Oh..." Amelie swallowed the instinct to dismiss the compliment. "Uh. Thank you."

"I like your yard."

"Yes." She stepped beside him. "Most of the plants come from friends. I've always liked that."

"I like that too. Well, should we go?" He checked his phone.

It seemed their time was running out fast. "Yes. Where do you want to have lunch? Should we try the pizzeria again?"

"Let's try something new. I saw a place that looked nice."

"Which one?"

"I can't remember the name, but I know how to get there."

They left the house and went to where he had parked his rental car. "I'm glad you ride with me now." He opened the door for her.

Amelie remembered how she'd driven herself to their first date. No. Meeting. It'd been a *meeting*. "Me too," she said and sat in the Toyota. She still had a lot of questions. She wanted to know more about what had happened in all the years they'd been out of touch. And she wanted to know more about him as a person. "Hey, Charlie?" she asked when he started the car.

"Yes?" He looked over his shoulder, checking for traffic.

"Do you think you'll come back to Bay Harbor now that you and Peter run the motel together?"

"It depends."

Amelie looked at her hands. "On what?"

"That depends too," he replied after a pause.

"Hmm." It wasn't a very definite answer, was it? "You don't want to tell me?"

"I'll tell you when I know," he said and glanced at her. "It mostly depends on you, I guess."

"Me?"

He flicked on the turn signal and turned. "Do you want me to come back, Amelie?"

"Well, sure. It would be nice to see you again."

He took another turn.

Amelie glanced out of the window, catching sight of slivers of blue wedged between houses. They were driving parallel to the sea.

"Let's say you won't be able to track down my letters to you," he said. "How would you feel then?"

Her blood suddenly felt cold in her veins. "Why? Are you saying you didn't send them after all?" Had he lied to her?

He slowed and looked at her. "I sent them. Every single one."

His eyes held nothing back as far as she could tell. "Okay." She inhaled.

"But what if you can't find them? What if they were destroyed or thrown away or...I don't know. I guess a hundred things can happen to a piece of unwanted paper."

Amelie looked out of the window again. How would she feel if none of the twenty-five letters he'd written ever materialized? Would she still believe him if she knew there was no chance of seeing proof his story was true? She cleared her throat. "I believe you, Charlie. I'm not going to lie; I'd like to see at least one of those letters. But if I don't, I still believe you."

He nodded and pulled to the curb, parking the car.

Amelie looked up. "That's the house I looked at," she said suddenly and pointed at it. "Remember Laurel at the pizzeria asking me about it? Her sister was my real estate agent."

"Yes, I remember. Kelly, wasn't it?"

"Yes, exactly. Laurel and Kelly." It was as beautiful as she remembered. In the back, the sea shimmered blue and inviting, framed by blooming hydrangeas and boxwood. But there was no restaurant here. "It's a residential street, Charlie." She turned to look at him. "We'll have to go back and turn left toward the harbor."

"I want a look at your house there. Do you have a minute?" Already, he was opening his door and getting out.

"*I* have a minute. But you don't. What happened to starving and all that?" She followed him.

He was waiting for her on the sidewalk. "How about we go check out the kitchen? Maybe there's food."

She looked left and right. "No? How about we don't do that. I'm not going to break in, Charlie."

"Let's go look in the windows. Nobody is living here, is there?"

"I'm not going to trespass any more than I'll break in. We need a real estate agent to go on the property. If you really want to sneak a look, I'll wait in the car. I'm too old for this."

He looked at her, and then he suddenly laughed.

"What now? What's so funny?" Amelie opened her hands. This was starting to annoy her.

"Nothing. You're right. I'm too old for it too." Charlie put a hand in his pocket and pulled out a key. "Luckily, we don't have to sneak." He handed her the key.

Amelie stared at it. "What is going on? What's this?"

"The key to your house."

"*My* house key? No, that's—" *In my purse*, she'd meant to say, but halfway through the sentence, the coin dropped. "The key to *that* house?" She pointed and raised her eyebrows in an unspoken question.

"Yes, that house. It's a goodbye gift for you." He ran a hand through his hair.

Peter does the same when he's nervous, Amelie thought randomly. She couldn't focus. "*That* house? The one over there?" she repeated, dumbfounded.

"Yes. It was supposed to be a surprise. That's the house you like, isn't it?"

"But it's... Wait, did you...*buy* it? No." She took a step back. She couldn't think when he was so close.

"Yes, of course I bought it." He tilted his head. "Are you mad?"

"I'm..." Again she looked at the key in her hand. It was a proper key.

"I bought the house as a gift for you, Amelie," he repeated. "I wanted to give you something before I leave."

She tilted her head as if her ear wasn't working. "You wanted to give me something, so you bought a really very expensive *house?*"

He tucked his chin. "Really very expensive is relative. Bay Harbor isn't exactly Sydney. I thought it was a bit of a steal, to be honest."

"I can't take a house from you, Charlie," Amelie said weakly.

"Well, the deed is in your name."

"I can't pay a mortgage, either." Her breathing started to quicken. What had Charlie gotten her into now?

He frowned. "Amelie, of course there's no mortgage. Why would I give you a house with a mortgage?"

"What?"

"It's not... I owe you more than a *house*," he said. "Come on. Let's go in and have a look, yeah? I really do have a plane to catch."

"Yeah," Amelie said slowly. "I need to sit down."

Charlie took the key from her and offered her his arm. Amelie took it. A feeling of unreality had settled on her. They walked to the front door, and Charlie pushed the key into the lock.

"How big is your ranch again?" Amelie asked. The key turned.

"Big enough." He opened the door. "After you."

"Big enough." She inhaled, and then she went inside.

The house greeted her like an old friend. It was just as beautiful as she remembered.

Behind her, Charlie closed the door. "Oh, I like it. Very nice." He came to stand beside her.

"You haven't even seen it before you bought it? Without a mortgage?" Amelie turned to him. "Just making sure."

He chuckled. "I wasn't the one who's going to live in it, was I?"

She didn't know what to say to that. "Look at the kitchen," she said finally.

They walked through the house room by room. Some of them, Amelie hadn't even seen last time. And with every room she saw, she fell deeper in love with the house.

Back in the living room, she sat on the couch.

"Are you okay?" Charlie asked and sat on the chair.

"I can't believe this is real."

"It's as real as the letters I sent. This is your house now, Amelie. You liked it, and you told me your mother is coming back. The old house used to be hers, and she'll probably be glad to have it back, don't you think? And you'll be glad to have your own."

"But a house is a huge purchase, Charlie. You don't owe me anything."

"I owe you a lot more than this. But that has nothing to do with the house." He leaned forward. "I just wanted you to have it. It's all settled. All that's left is for you to say yes. Say yes?"

"Yes, but..."

"But?"

"But you have to come back," she whispered. "I want you to be here, not in Sydney."

He looked down, and when he met her eyes again, his face had changed. "Then I'll come back. If you want me here, I'll come back to Bay Harbor."

Amelie's heart sped up, drumming on her lungs and making it hard to breathe. "I mean... I don't mean..."

"No, I know. I realize that." He made a move as if he was going to take her hand. "That's not what I meant, either. But you want me to just be in Bay Harbor, yes?"

Amelie's head swam. What sort of responsibility was she— "Yes," her mouth said. She slapped a hand over it. "You have to decide for yourself," she said, too late.

"Oh, I will," Charlie said. The lines in the corners of his eyes deepened. "It's not like it hasn't occurred to me."

"Don't come because of me," Amelie said. She had to say it, but the words sounded all wrong to her ears. She wanted Charlie in her life, not in Sydney. She *wanted* him to come because of her.

"I make my own decisions," he said softly. "Always have, always will. Don't worry, Amelie. If I move here, I'll buy my own house. You can't make me do anything I don't want to do anyway." He rubbed a hand over his chin. "Maybe we can be friends. And maybe I can get to know my son."

Amelie nodded, relieved. "I would like that."

Charlie's phone beeped. He checked the screen. Then he reached out and, for a moment, let his hand rest on hers. "I have to go. Kelly has all the papers you need, and she'll meet you at your old house now. You can move today if you like. And when I come back, we'll have that lunch we missed."

"Maybe you can tell me more about yourself then," Amelie said. She didn't want him to leave. "I think there's still some blank patches in your story I'd like to fill in."

"I have more questions for you too."

"Do you think we might try the phone thing one more time?"

He smiled. "We've definitely waited long enough for technology to work out the kinks. Peter has my number, and I have to admit I made him give me yours."

They stood. Charlie pressed his lips together in a thin line. And then, as if he had lost an internal battle, he exhaled a tight breath and held out his hand.

Amelie took it. It was large and warm and still a perfect fit for her own. Holding it felt good—and much more familiar than it should. "Friends," she promised bravely.

"Friends," he repeated and then he led her out of the house and back to the car.

CHAPTER 32

"Peter?" Mela squinted into the dark and lowered her duffle bag onto the sofa. It was late, and night had fallen some time ago. Already, summer was turning into fall and the days were shorter. "Are you all right?"

"I was waiting for you. I fell asleep." Peter stood and switched on the lamp on the night table. He had a crease on the cheek and his hair was ruffled. "How is Sunny?"

"She's exhausted from the drive but better than expected. She claims she's already in less pain than she was before the surgery."

"And how are you?" He came to her. "Long time no see, stranger."

"I'm all right as well. Glad to be home." She put her arms around his neck, and he pulled her to him. She'd missed him so much. "Where is everyone?"

Peter let go. "Everyone's asleep."

"Kimmie texted me the bad news." Mela shook her head. "I was hoping she would stay longer. Well, for now...can you help Sunny inside? She has a walker, but the step will be difficult."

"Sure." He stepped into his shoes. "Is she on pain meds?"

"She took something for the drive, but she thinks she'll be okay. Of course, there's also a lot of physical therapy coming for her. We'll have to see how it goes."

They went outside, and Peter helped Sunny out of the car. "Welcome back, Sunny." He enveloped her in a bear hug. "You did it. I'm so proud of you."

"So far, so good," she murmured, drowsy from the late hour and medication. "I'm ready to lie down though. Help me get inside, Peter."

Mela followed the pair with their bags. The flowers in the front yard scented the air even at night, and the stars shone brightly.

A bureaucratic snag at the hospital had kept them late. But Sunny insisted on getting home instead of staying another day, and even though Mela didn't like driving at night, now she was glad she gave in to her aunt. It was much nicer to be back in Bay Harbor than to be sleeping on a cot in the hospital.

She tucked Sunny in and sat down at the side of her bed. "Pretty soon you can move into a proper bedroom upstairs, my dear. Do you have everything you need for now?"

"More than that," Sunny murmured, her eyes closed. Despite being half asleep, her fingers searched for Mela's hand. "More than that."

"Good night, then." Mela gently squeezed her hand. "Dream of the beach walk you'll be taking soon."

"Mmmh."

Mela smiled and left, softly closing the door behind her.

The kitchen was dark and quiet, and so was the living room. She found Peter outside, sitting in one of the wicker chairs. He turned when he heard her.

"Come sit for a moment."

She did. On her chair was a thick knitted throw. And in the light of the citronella candle, she spotted a white wine on the table. "I'm too tired to drink," she sighed.

"That's fine," he said. "Let's just sit and watch the stars. Unless you want to go to bed?"

"I'm too keyed up to sleep too," she admitted. "Come to think of it, maybe I'll have a glass after all. It's a beautiful night, isn't it?"

"I do like that night-blooming jasmine." He stood to pour their wine, handing her a glass.

"And the rushing of the sea."

"Cheers, my love. You did a fantastic job." He lifted his glass to meet hers. Before he drank, he leaned over and kissed her lips.

"Cheers." She took a sip of the cool, clean wine and then rested her head on the back of the chair so she could see the night sky.

"Are you cold?"

"I'm fine." The air was warm, and the stars clearly visible. There were so many of them. It was so late, the moon was already dipping toward the tops of the pine trees.

"Sisley and Lovie are asleep upstairs," Peter said after a while. "Kimmie and Johanna are at Kimmie's house."

"Kimmie called. The girls will move into her house, but I hope she'll come back soon."

He nodded. "I'm sure her work can be as long or short as she wants to make it."

Mela looked at him. "Do you know if anything happened? I mean for her to suddenly head out on an assignment like that?"

In the flickering candlelight, she could see Peter frown. "I don't. I wonder if she and Sisley got in a fight over Bennett?"

"I doubt it. Sisley isn't interested. At least, she doesn't want to be. And Kimmie... To tell you the truth, I'm not sure she's moved on from the divorce yet."

"Maybe that's it, then. I feel like there might've been a text or a call, maybe. She didn't say, and I didn't want to pry."

Mela pressed her lips together. Kimmie hadn't told her, but she'd make sure to ask before her daughter left. "I have to trust she'll be smart about it."

"She's certainly smart," Peter agreed. "She'll take care of herself."

"Have you talked to Charlie?"

"He arrived home safe and sound." Peter turned his head, and Mela saw a smile in his eyes. "To be honest, I expect he'll be back soon."

"You think?"

"Yeah. Have you talked with Amelie yet?"

"She called." Mela sat up in her chair. "What a gift. Unbelievable."

"He was glad she accepted it," Peter said. "I felt his relief when he told me. For a moment there he was scared he'd overstepped."

"How big *is* his ranch in Australia?" Mela asked casually.

"It's big," Peter said.

"How big?"

He grinned. "*Big* big. He didn't give me numbers, but I'm no fool."

She smiled. "So the renovations will go forward?"

Peter nodded. "He insisted on paying for them. It's his buy-in into the partnership." His wicker chair crackled as he shifted his weight. "Maybe we'll get the motel back in shape after all."

"That would be great. I hope he'll come back sometime."

"Oh, he'll be back. You know he's still carrying a torch for your friend. And he's a dad now. Yeah—he'll be back."

"Amelie wants to see Charlie again. So would Bennett, from what she said."

"Yes. I talked with him, and he seems fine with his new dad. It kills me he's known for years I was his uncle and never said a word." Peter chuckled quietly. "There's another smart one for you."

"All our kids are so clever." Mela's cell phone buzzed. Reflexively, she pulled it from her pocket and checked the screen. "Oh." She let her phone sink again.

"What? What happened?"

"Talking about clever—it's my son, Morris. He's on his way to Bay Harbor."

"He's going to visit? When?"

Mela squinted at the sky. The stars were still glowing, but over the sea, their light was dimming. Soon, the sun would rise to dip the sky in all the bright colors of a late summer morning. "Today," she said. "And he's bringing his piano."

"Oh! Electric?"

She looked at the texts again. "He's coming in a truck. So…I think it's more than just a keyboard. It won't even go through the door!"

Peter set his glass down. "He can put it in the dining room in the motel," he said. "There's space for several pianos. Pianists, too."

"Right." Mela emptied her glass and snuggled down, pulling the soft throw over her. Peter moved his chair beside hers and put his arm around her shoulders. She rested her head on it, her eyes on the last rays of moonlight that played in silvery streaks on the dark sea.

"So much going on." He kissed her hair. "Are we ever going to sail into calm waters?"

"This is our calm water," she murmured. "This is our perfect."

For a long while, they sat, watching the night dim and the moon sink. The candle burned out, and still it was lighter than before.

"I think that's the sunrise." Peter yawned. "Look at us, staying up all night."

Mela sat up and stretched. "A new day, a new adventure. Morris will be here in a few hours. And I want time with Kimmie before she leaves."

He stood and held out a hand. "I promised Amelie and Bennet to help with the move. How about we try and get some rest before everything starts?"

She took his hand and smiled. "Never a dull moment in Bay Harbor."

Don't miss what happens next in Bay Harbor! *Seaside Rumors* continues the stories of families and friends as together they tackle old secrets and new beginnings with humor, heart, and lots of hope.

THE BEACH COVE SERIES

Escape with Maisie to charming Beach Cove and meet a wonderful cast of friends, families, and unique characters. The beaches are warm and inviting, the sea bluer than it has any right to be, and the small town is brimming with secrets. Maisie and her three best friends take turns helping each other through emotional trials, bittersweet mysteries, and mistakes of the heart. For the free prequel to the series, go to https://BookHip.com/KMSQRTT

Beach Cove Home

Beach Cove Inn

Beach Cove Sisters

Beach Cove Secrets

The Bay Harbor Series

Visit the seaside in the small town of Bay Harbor, meet new friends, and lose yourself in the riveting saga of strong women building happy lives. Feel like you are right beside them as you walk quaint streets smelling of salt water taffy, browse cute stores for that elusive perfect swimsuit, and skip over the beach toward the sea because the sand is too hot. Most of all, find out how mothers and daughters, friends and families help each other overcome challenges and solve bittersweet secrets.

Seaside Friends

Seaside Sunrise

Seaside Rumors

ABOUT THE AUTHOR

Nellie Brooks writes heartwarming women's fiction with relatable characters who face challenges ranging from bitter to sweet. After years of traveling the world and studying the behavior of animals (that appear in her stories), she turned to writing fiction. Her books are set in Maine, where Nellie likes to spend time on the beach with her family. Visit www.nelliebrooks.com to subscribe to her newsletter and find out more.

Made in the USA
Coppell, TX
21 July 2023

19453694R00142